Moore Lies Unveiled

Florencia Flo

Andrea Johnson Books Publishing

Moore Lies Unveiled

Cover art designed by Andrea Johnson.

First published by Andrea Johnson Books Publishing. 5/7/2022

6565 N. MacArthur Blvd, Suite 225 Dallas, TX. 75039
www.Ajbpublishing.com

This is a work of fiction. Names, characters, places and incidents either are a product of the author's imagination, or used fictitiously. Any resemblance to actual persons, living or dead, events or locales, is entirely coincidental.

Because of the dynamic nature of the Internet, any web addresses or links contained in this book may have changed since publication and may no longer be valid. The views expressed in this work are solely those of the author and do not necessarily reflect the views of the publisher, and the publisher herby disclaims any responsibility for them.

ISBN: 978-0-578-36255-7

Acknowledgements

God put in my heart to use my gift of creative writing as a way to express myself; he also encouraged me not to give up when I would start to doubt myself. I knew there were so many other great authors already out there, and I wondered how my story would stand out amongst them. But he said leave that up to me. My journey started Dec. 22 and on the 28th I was done, or so I thought. He guided me to so many options that had me feeling discouraged of the process just to have it published, that I gave up, but he never allowed me to forget about what I started.

I remember reading another great story on Wattpad.com and again he said to me; why are you still reading great stories when you already have one ready? It just needs a little more detail to make it great; so I went back and did a complete revise. When there was nothing more for me to do to it; he had me reach out to fellow Author J-Deck for tips to help me with how to do edits as well as kept me motivated. It was through his page that I found my publisher and consultant that was inspired by my passion, dedication and uniqueness of my writing style that she and her staff gave life to my baby, Moore Lies Unveiled.

I wanna give a great thanks to Andrea Johnson and everyone who had a hand in making me an Author at Andrea Johnson Books Publishing. I may not know your names but when you see this, you'll know I'm talking about you; thank you for your patience when it came to making the cover and all the hard work y'all put into it.

I want to also give thanks to my aunt Louisa King and Jocelyn Allen, Beatrice Suggs, Nadine Williams and Marie Dabney; for being the mother figures that God put in my life after my biological mother Florence Novella Allen-Grays died. Each one of you had a piece of her and I truly thank God for your words of wisdom, love, compassion and impacts you each had in my life.

Tabitha Gaston, my sisters through Christ TasiaTae "MsKeepItClassy, Katrina McCullough, Telisha Starks, Jaleesa Bray, My HannaBearey, Brittney Allen, Kimberly Sam and Jomika Williams.

Lastly but most important my Son Va'Lad Grays, psychiatrist Mr. Jeffrey Russell, brother through Christ Sione and the only person from day one saw me as brother, friend and child of her own Xenia Steed. Each one of you was a branch and root in my life that kept me afloat; you were each a milestone in my life that if it wasn't for one of you, I don't know how I would have made it because God made sure you were there for me at the time I needed you. As a new chapter in my life opens as Author Florencia Flo, thank you, ShainaB, and the many others from my Facebook family:

@ facebook.com/Shonnea.G.

Twitter Friends @AFlorenciaFlo/ Author Florencia Flo.

Thank you all for your support and encouragement towards my journey as a new Authoress.

Thank you All and have a Blessed Day

Moore Lies Unveiled

Florencia Flo

Part 1 -

Secrets

Chapter One

X'avian's POV

This morning I woke up with this eerie feeling that something bad has or is about to happen. I've been feeling this way since my 18th birthday; the day when I had an argument with my mom about why my dad was not being around in my life. I still haven't been able to shake it off; so, instead I'm just going to brush it off my shoulder like it doesn't bother me at all.

"X'avian get up, it's time for school!" I hear my mom slightly yelling as I slowly wake up from a long night's rest.

"I'm up Mom! There's no need to yell!" I tell her as I stretch my arms above my head and sit upright in bed. Man, she gets on my damn nerve when she does that. It's enough I really hate this damn school; they're fake as fuck for one, and they're all snooty, uppity-ass sons of bitches.

I begin to start my day off with a quick shower, basic hygiene, and pin my dreads back in a ponytail. I don't bother adding swag to my school uniform because it only causes me to get in trouble for trying. So, after checking myself over in the mirror, I grab my book bag and keys as I head downstairs.

Me and my mom live in a huge two-bedroom single family townhouse; I think it's a bit much, but she wants to live like the Joneses because she a bit on the Booshie side; thanks to my grandparents; she was born and raised in the ghetto, but after my grandpa's promotion and finding out she was pregnant with me, he moved his family to the north side of Chicago.

As I head downstairs, I instantly get that eerie feeling again, I still can't put my finger on it. I have this really bad feeling in my gut that it's something really serious. But I shake it off as soon as I see my mom in the kitchen; finishing up breakfast.

"Morning, mom!"

She yelled from the kitchen when she heard me coming down the stairs.

"Oh my God! It's going to rain. I can't believe you're actually leaving on time today!" She said, joking to me as she gave me a kiss on the cheek.

"Whatever; I'm always going to be on time now that I don't have to ride that slow, stinky, and overcrowded-ass-bus; I have a car now!" I responded a little cocky at the end, while dangling my keys in the air to the car she bought for me on my eighteenth birthday.

"I promised you that when you become a senior, I was going to get you a car." My mom said with a smirk.

"Thank you so much mom! But I have to go before I end up being late." I tell her in a rushed tone, as I kissed her on the cheek.

"Ok baby! Have a good-day at school. Stay out of trouble and I'll see you when I get home from work." She said as she walked from the kitchen towards me.

"Ok, bye!" She says as she gives me a kiss on the cheek and I swear I felt as if it was more than just a 'see you' later kiss, but again, I brushed it off and headed out the door to school.

*Kenda's POV**

I felt as though I should have said more to him before he left. I am planning on it tonight, when he comes from school and after I get home from work, to tell him about his father. Even though I'll be going against my father's wishes; but don't-ask-me-why I feel something bad may come of it afterwards. So, I brush-it-off; thinking it's me being nervous of finally-telling-X'avian about his father's absence; perhaps that is the obvious reason as to why-I-am feeling nervous.

I decide not to give it a second thought and I head back into the kitchen to finish eating breakfast. I put away the dishes once I'm done washing them and finishing off the kitchen: by wiping down the counters and the stove. I then quickly head back upstairs to make sure I have everything before I leave for work, but realize once I walked into my bedroom that I almost left without my cellphone.

I place my cell phone in my purse and check-myself-again in-my-full-length mirror; with my Chanel bag hanging-off-my-arm. I then head downstairs to leave out-the-door-for work. I get into my 2015 Jaguar, press the start button, buckle up and pull out the driveway after placing it in gear.

It doesn't take me long to get to work and since I'm a little early, I actually have time to stop for a cup of coffee at the gas station. I pull in the parking lot and see that it's not really busy. So, I decide to leave it running; the car automatically locks when I have the key sensor on me.

"Morning!" I casually greet the store clerk as I walk-in heading to the-coffee-machine to make me a hot-cup-of-Joe.

I grab a medium-size-cup, filling it up just-a-few-inches below the brim; then-I-proceed to make it the-way-I-like: loads-of-cream; making-it-turn-almost a pale white, and four shakes of sugar from-the-container and I use the stir-straws to stir-it; before adding the sippy-top.

As I head-to-the-counter, I pull out my card from my Chanel wallet that matches my purse to pay for my coffee.

"That'll be $3.65." The store clerk tells me after he rings up my coffee.

"Ok, here you go."

I respond as I give him my debit card to pay for the coffee. He swipes my card and hands it back to me with the receipt. I stuff-my-card back in my wallet and drop-it-in my purse as I take my first sip of coffee and pay-no-mind to the guy standing outside the gas-station's door in front of my car. I barely open the door; when I hear a deep-voice yelling at me saying:

"GET-THE-FUCK-OUT-THE-DAMN CAR, BITCH!" The voice of the man I recognized standing outside the gas station doors, yells in my face while blocking me from closing my car door.

"Please; don't hurt me!"

I respond with fear laced in my voice that I didn't recognize as my own.

"SHUT-THE-FUCK-UP! BITCH!" The man yells as he pulls out a gun and points it at my face as I try to comply with his demands.

"HURRY-THE-FUCK UP! YOU'RE MOVING-TOO-FUCKING SLOW!" The man yells again more aggressively, as he holds his finger firmly on the trigger and points the gun at my chest now.

"Please, take everything!" I say, as I shove my purse in his direction and try to yell "HELP!"- Just before he pulled the trigger and shot me in the chest.

POW!!! The sound of his gun going off throws me in a state of shock because at first, I am unaware that I'm shot; it happened so fast; I didn't even realize he had dragged me from my car, until my body slams against the pavement and the guy was fleeing in my car as I lay on the ground, motionless with my eyes closed.

I can now feel myself slipping away and like a projector in rewind, my life actually flashes before my eyes, only showing the happiest moments of my life.

The day I met Laronzo in high school, us making love, the moment I found out I was pregnant, giving birth to X'avian, his first words, his first steps, his first potty, his first day of school and then finally this morning.

13

I feel a tear slip from my eyes as I remember the kiss on the cheek, I gave him. "X'avian, I'm sorry I didn't tell you earlier about your father," is really what that kiss meant. Because I was going to tell him about his father when he came home from school, against my father's wishes.

I pause at that exact moment as I feel my body getting cold and my chest rise one last time, with the thought that I actually died with my family's secret.

Cassius Moore's POV

Ring!!! Ring!!! The phone rings twice before I finally pick up.

"Hello!" I say once I answer the phone, hoping to hear some good news.

"Boss, it's done!" The person responded once they heard my voice.

"Ok, take the car to a chop shop, ditch the phone, and go incognito till this blows over. If you get caught, you bettah not bring up my name or else I'll have someone pay your family a visit!"

I tell him as I give him strict instructions and a warning that I hope he took heed to. Because once that nigga Ghost find out about Kenda's death, because he has a fucking nose like a greyhound; he won't rest till he finds this nigga and put him behind bars; that's why I hired an out of town nigga to do the job and if he did it right, his ass won't get found by this nigga.

"Got you, Boss. I'm already."

Chapter Two

Still from Cassius' POV

Eight hours later....

After getting everything settled with my daughter, I decided to wait for my bastard grandson to get out of school to tell him about his mother.

I told her to stay away from those McTyson boys, but she didn't listen; the whore literally slept with the enemy's son. I despised her for that and fed her lies that he'll never be for their son. My damn nephew had to undo what I did and convince her to tell X'avian the truth.

Now she can take it to her grave and I'll just have Tate to worry about later. I'll show him what happens to those who can't keep their mouths shut, by ruining what he loves the most.

I worked too hard to get where I am for her to involve herself with that bastard again.

"X'avian, can you please come home ASAP!"

I say in a text message that I sent him, as I sit on the couch in my daughter's house, with my wife and nephew, who decides he wanna come back around when he hears about the death of my daughter, as we wait for my Bastard grandson to arrive. I hope my nephew ain't come back to stir up more damn trouble now that's she gone, and I hope he's here to keep that Bastard child of hers in check.

"Baby, how could they take her from us?" My wife sobs in my arms as I hold her while rubbing her back.

"I'll get the bastard who did this and make him pay; I am not the police commissioner for nothing." I tell her, while trying to sound as sincere as possible, as I begin to cry myself because of the actions she made me take.

** Tate's POV**

Look at his ass, playing like he really gives a fuck. He's a fucking monster. I know he had something to do with her death, just like he did with my father and mother's. Soon as I talk with my lawyer, I'm getting custody of my nephew, so he won't be next. I lift my head to see who I assume is my nephew coming in the front door with a confused look on his face, as he looks me up and down. I haven't seen him since my dad and sister forced me out of his life at the age of three.

"Grandpa, what's up? And who is he?"

X'avian asked as he looks away from me to his grandfather for answers, because he doesn't recognize who I am.

"Son, sit down." His grandfather responds nonchalantly.

"What's going on, why is Grandma crying?"

He asked as he noticed my mother sobbing hysterically on the couch.

"Xav, come sit down."

I spoke up suddenly to him. Referring to the nickname I gave him when he was young, as I motioned for him to come sit next to me on the couch. But he refused my offer, going and sitting next to my mother instead on the opposite side.

Carlene Moore's POV

I haven't seen my son since X'avian was three and all of a sudden, he shows up out of nowhere; something really isn't right.

"Your mom was shot today on her way to work; she died on the scene." Cassius said in a clipped voice.

So much for easing into it and allowing it all to sink in. My husband can be so inconsiderate sometimes.

"No, this can't be true!" My grandson says in disbelief to his grandfather, as tears brim at the bottom of his eyes.

Before I can move closer to console him, he jumps up from the couch and rushes out the door with his keys in his hand. I run behind him, but by the time I reach the door, he's already in his car and down the street.

"Damn Cassius, did you really have to be that heartless and say it so bluntly!" I yelled in his face once I made it back to the house.

"What? I had no other way to say it!" He responded unphased by my tone, with a hint of amusement in the end. Like he meant to say it how he did, heartless and cold.

"Shut up! Just shut the fuck up!"

I yelled at him in frustration as I turned to my son Tate and spoke harshly.

"Get the fuck up Lavon Tate and find him! And when you do, I think it's best he stays with you."

I say to him, as he gets up from the couch to go search for my grandson. I slightly stepped in his path and leaned closer to him to whisper the last part in his ear.

"Ok mom, I'm already on it."

He whispered back to me as I give a hug to the man that I raised since the age of one. He shook his head as he turned and whispered to my husband as he headed out the door.

"All secrets unfold at some point, you know?"

He then headed out the door to look for my grandson. He searched for two hours only to find him back at home in his mother's bed, crying.

Chapter Three

Two months later....

X'avian's POV

Man, life-is-fucked-up! I now live with my uncle and today is my first day at my new school. I decide to keep my prep-school look, but instead I give it a little hood-swag since this school doesn't require seniors to wear uniforms.

Now that my mom's gone, nobody in the streets will know me by X'avian because I am now going by my street name, Vicious, because the moment my mom died; I became a cold-hearted, no love for no mutha-fucking body type nigga.

Ayranea's POV

"Ayranea Jenkins, it's time to get your ass up for school. Get up now!"

I lazily throw the covers from over my tired body, pulling myself in the upright position with my back against my headboard, as an attempt to show her I'm about to get up.

She turns to leave, but quickly turns back around like she forgot to tell me something, almost catching me mid-stride as I was about to lay back down, but I play it off by stretching my arms above my head.

"Oh, and please get your sister up on time so she isn't late again for daycare."

She yells again before she turns back around from my bedroom and heads down the hallway to the front door for work. I dramatically sigh out loud, but this time, I wait until I hear her leave out the front door and lock it behind her. I listen until I hear her 2015 BMW back out the driveway and her engine faze in the distance, as she drives farther away from the house before I get comfortable under my blanket, so I can rest for about an hour to start my day.

The school I go to is just a block away and the daycare is right across the street from it. I honestly think she does-that-shit to get on my fucking nerves, but then again, it could be to make sure we leave on time. I already have my alarm clock set for 7:30; it's now 6:45. I yawn tiredly and instantly fall back asleep as soon as my head falls back on the pillow.

BEEP! BEEP!! BEEP!!! BEEP!!!! I am wakened out of my sleep once again by the beeping of my alarm.

I sit up again this time a little more energized; I stretch my arms high above my head while dragging my legs over the side of the bed.

As I proceed to stand up to stretch my entire body; my feet get tangled in the covers, and get dragged with me, causing it to fall on the floor. I pick them up from the ground and then started to make my bed before I turn to walk into my adjoined bathroom. Making sure to take care of my hygiene and take a quick shower, getting myself ready for school. Once I finish, I head over to my closet to pick an outfit to wear to school.

Thank God this year I am a senior so I can wear regular damn clothes and not those ratchet ass uniforms. So, today, I'm wearing a simple hooded, half shirt that shows off my belly ring, with matching joggers, and wedged Tim's boots to make it all pop.

"Yes, a bitch gotta look fly!" I playfully say out loud while snapping my finger in the air as I use my favorite RuPaul quote: "And what!!!" I know I sound horrible, but that's the best imitation I can come up with. Ok, enough playing around. I head over to the mirror to do my makeup next.

My face is flawless, so I don't need to apply too much; all I put on is: mascara, eyeliner, and lip gloss to make these juicy ass lips pop. I pop my lips together to even out the coating so it looks perfect. Then I head over to my sister, Kyn'Asia's room to get her ready for school.

I know you're wondering why I haven't mentioned my father yet; well, that's a different story for a different day. So, I'll give you the watered-down version. Plain and simple, my dad is a man whore and decided I would be better off living with my stepmother in good ole windy city Chicago. I hope you catch the sarcasm, but he wanted to whore around without worrying about little ole me. I know you like my little ole southern belle voice I used when I said the last part.

"Asia, get up momma!" I coo at her as I gently tap her leg until she starts to wake up.

"I don't wanna go to school!" She whines in her little cute baby voice. She sounds so precious for a four-year-old.

"Awe, come on, sweet cheeks. It's almost 8 o'clock and if we're late again, they will call Mom."

I said to influence her to get up faster, and it actually worked like a charm. She jumped up out of bed, throwing the covers from over her like someone lit firecrackers under her little ass. I shake my head as I burst out laughing as she races to her bathroom to take care of her hygiene. When she's finally done, she comes out with her cute Hello Kitty bathrobe. I helped her get dressed in the outfit I picked out for her. Then I hand her shoes so she can put them on like a big girl.

"I'm ready, Nea!" She says to me after putting her shoes on the wrong feet.

"Hmm! Since when did you get two left feet?" I say jokingly while showing her the peace sign to indicate the number two.

"Oops!" She says as she takes them off again; this time putting her shoes on the correct feet.

When she's done, I grab her hand and gently drag her to my room to get my bag and keys off my nightstand. I pick her up, putting her on my hip, then jog down the hallway to the front door to head out to drop her off at the daycare, and then off to Ratchet High. It only takes a few minutes to get there and it's now 8:10; I have ten minutes to get her signed in.

"Nea, will you let me go to Tashie house after school?" She begs as she tries to give me her best puppy dog eyes, pleading with me to say yes.

I sigh before giving her my answer: "Sure, why not!" She jumps up and down joyfully; you would swear she's my child instead of my damn sister from the way she acts.

Finally, we arrive at Kendall Learning Center; Asia lets go of my hand as soon as we walk through the double doors. She runs off to her group and sits next to her BFF Tashie. I know she already told her about staying over at her house after school because they both come running full speed back to me.

"Thank you, Miss Nea. I'll tell my mom she's coming home with us today after school." Tashie says to me in the cutest little voice ever while hugging my legs.

"You're welcome. Just tell your mom to text me when she's ready to drop her off, ok, Hun?" She nods her head in response as they both give me one last hug before skipping back to their group again.

Finally, I got the chance to sign her in on time.

"Later, Mrs. Berkman!" I politely say to the secretary sitting at the front desk as I head out to this boring, ghetto, and ratchet ass school. I sigh dramatically as I cross the street and notice my best friend jogging up the sidewalk towards me.

"Heyyyy, bitch!" Demeekia's loud mouth ass yells while waving her hand in the air like I didn't see her.

"What's up, bitch? Damn you looking flier than me, bitch!" I say as a compliment, because she has on a bright Indonesia pattern, v-cut romper top that wraps around the neck and zips up in the back with black bottoms. Like I said, ghetto ass school with classy ass bitches.

"So, did you finish up what we had for homework last night?" She asks as we walk side by side up the steps leading to the main hallway of the school.

"Bitch, of course I did. You know it's a must I keep my GPA up, bitch, especially if I'm trying to get the fuck away from this ratchet bitch!"

I say with a little booshie attitude as I refer to our high school at the end.

"Yeah! Bitch, I feel you. I'm trying to do the same shit, ya feel me!" She responds while snapping her finger at the end. We continue making small talk as we reach the double doors of the school.

Once inside, we headed to our locker, which is on opposite ends of the main hallway, so we had to part ways until the third and fourth period.

"Well, bitch, I'll see you in the third block. Don't forget your fucking project that you stashed in my damn locker last week!" I say to her before we head to our lockers.

"Bitch, bring it with you. Your damn second block is closer to your fucking locker than mine is any damn way. You act like you'll be going out your way; literally you pass it on your way to third block." She responds in a ghetto manner while rolling her neck at me teasingly before turning and walking away to the right, heading to her locker.

"Bitch, you better be fucking lucky you my fucking BFF or else I would be whooping your ass right now for talking to me like that!" I yell back at her, making her laugh and flip me the bird as she jogs a little faster. I chuckle to myself as I turn around, not paying attention to who's behind me.

I instantly bump into a six feet tall, medium chocolate tone, prep dressed nigga, who added his own swag to it, with neatly kept dreads that reach just below his neck in a ponytail, and a firm rock-hard chest. It throws me off balance, almost causing me to fall.

"Whoa, lil momma, watch yourself!" He says as he catches me by the arm before I can fall on my ass.

"Too busy being a ratchet ass bitch to pay attention to where the fuck you're going!" He responds as he helped me regain my balance.

'*No-the-fuck-this-nigga* didn't just call me a RATCHET BITCH!' I think to myself while getting pissed off at the same time, as I snatched my arm away from him while getting in his face on my tippy toes.

"Who the fuck are you to call me a RATCHET BITCH, MOTHERFUCKER!" I yell back at him while poking him in his chest as I speak every word.

He simply shoves me away from him, unphased by my reaction, and replies all nonchalant. "I'm just calling it how I see it."

"Really!" I respond back, dumbfounded, while not realizing the ooooohs and aahhs coming from other students that were crowded around us.

He brushes past me before I can respond back to his flip at the mouth remark; so instead I turn my attention towards the crowd.

"What the fuck y'all oohing for? Don't get it twisted, bitches!" I yell at everyone standing around in the hall; they all scurry away like the scared little bitches they've always been.

"Yeah! I thought so." I mumble under my breath, as I continue on towards my locker.

See, bitches know not to fuck with me. Yeah, I'm 5'2, but I'm also that bitch who will get up in your ass if you try messing with me or anyone I'm close to. So, whoever that preppy ass nigga is, he must be new to mess with the Queen B of this school.

Yeah, I'm a classy bitch, but I'm also that bitch whose bad side you don't want to be on or fuck with.

Chapter Four

** *Vicious' POV***

Damn shawty was fine as hell but feisty as fuck forreal-forreal. For a minute I thought she was about to whoop my ass for calling her ratchet; don't get me wrong I ain't no scary nigga by far. Shit, but if looks could kill; I'll damn sure be six feet under. So, nigga like me know how to maintain my cool. But I already know I can pull her if I want just by the way she was eyeing a nigga chest. Yeah, I'm a cocky nigga but I can back that shit up if any bitch wanna try me.

'Man just that fucking quick I forgot where the fuck the office at bruh.' I think to myself while I wander round all stupid since shawty got my head all fucked up now.

"Ahh excuse me Ma'am; can you direct me to the office please if you don't mind?" I ask while licking my lips at this fine ass redbone chick with a tight red button up shirt; that's unbuttoned at the bust line and a pencil skirt that damn near look painted on, before she could pass me.

"Oh sure hun! It's not a problem at all." She responded, sounding all sexy and shit.

"You're actually almost there; just continue on down this hall and it's about three more doors down between two big glass windows on either side of it. You can't miss it because it says 'office' on the door if it's open." She responds as she pointed with her index finger toward the same direction I was headed.

"Thank you, Ma'am! Are you a teacher here?" I ask her before she can walk away.

"Oh, you must be new, but yes I am." She says to me a lil dumbfounded by my question as she gives me a quick once over and she licks her lips, while thinking I didn't notice her flirtatious gesture. *'Damn is it that obvious?'* I think to myself. I just nod my head instead of giving her a verbal response.

"Thank you Missss"...I prolong the end hoping she catch on that I'm asking about her name.

"Oh, I'm sorry; it's *Mrs.* Carter!" She emphasizes Mrs.; like I give a fuck if she married. Fuck! She might be old, but I'll still give her ass the biznizz while she flirting with a nigga like me; shit!

"Well nice to meet you Mrs. Carter!" I emphasize back to her with a wink, causing her to blush as she walks away. Fuck! She might be old, but I'll give her ass the biznzz while she flirting with a nigga like me! Shid.

Yeah, buddy I hope I get whatever class she teaches cause that ass (emphasizes) is mine bruh.

Just by the way her firm and juicy her ass jiggle up and down as she walks down the hall to her class; got a nigga 'D' twitching and shit! (literally) Snapping myself out my daze moment and putting my attention back to what I'm suppose to be doing;

"Oh yeah!" I'm supposed to be going to the office. I remind myself as I turn slowly around making sure I don't bump into anyone like lil miss shawty did me this morning.

Damn look how quick she popped back in my head making me forget about miss watcha name. I snap my finger as I try to remember the redbone teacher's name from just a few minutes ago. Man fuck it! It'll come to me later bruh when I see her again. Finally, I make it to the office just as the damn tardy bell rings.

"Fuck!" I mumble under my breath knowing; I'm about to stand out in class as the preppy new kid with swag.

"Bruh ya slipping my nigga!" My self-consciousness yells at me in my head.

"Excuse me; can I please get my schedule and tardy slip so I can head to my class?" I say to the Secretary at the front desk slightly with an attitude.

"Mhmm jus'tah a damn minute!" She replied with an even harder attitude. Shocking the fuck out me because she doesn't look like the cussing type.

So, I decided to just let that shit slide cause; from the looks of it I can tell her day already fucked up. So instead, I turn and take a seat in one of the empty chairs in front of her desk.

"Um what's your name Hun?" She asks a lil nicer I guess because I didn't give her an attitude back; which I'm thankful for.

"Oh! yes Ma'am, it's umm X'avian McTyson-Moore but my uncle dropped Moore from my name and registered me under McTyson." I responded explaining why I had two last names.

"So, you're registered only as McTyson; correct"?

"Yes Ma'am!"

"Hmm McTyson, McTyson; oh, there you are. You must have an older brother here." She asks me while making me look dumbfounded for a second.

34

Her whole expression changes as quick as mine after realizing; I have no clue who the hell she talking about but; I'll play this shit out just to see who this nigga is carrying my last name.

"Oh yeah I forgot he enrolled at the beginning of school; I went with my grandparent and mom. We got separated due to a bad divorce and my dad took my brother to stay with him after the divorce was finalized, because he was older. But since my mom died a few months ago my uncle took me in and transferred me here because this is the school I'm zoned for."

I respond back to her without any hesitation and mentally pat myself on the back for quickly coming up with a convincing lie, because I can literally see the relief wash over her face; like she just knew she opened up a can of worms and she doesn't realize how right she is.

"Well, here is your schedule, just tell your brother Darian to show you around since y'all have first and third block together." She says with a bit of relief as she holds out my class schedule. I mentally fist bump myself for how easy I got her to spill the beans.

"Thank you, Ma'am and trust me I will." I respond with a smile and a smirk on my face which I'm glad she didn't catch it because I manage to cover it up with my million-dollar smile. That causes her to blush as I take me my schedule and tardy slip for class from her hand, while taking a moment to look at what classes I have. I notice it also has my locker number and combo on it and a map of the school on back leading from the office.

"Well, I guess I should get going; have a nice day Ma'am!" I politely say to her as I turn to leave deciding to head to my locker first.

As I follow the map leading to the hallway where my locker would be. I look until I find 118 so I can dump off what I don't. I need to get rid of the unnecessary shit that's weighing my ass down.

After finally finding which one it is; I put in my combo number as it opens it with ease and throw everything in it except for a binder and pen that I know I will need.

I then shut it tight, and I pull on it to make sure that it's closed securely and then slowly walk to my first hour class.

"Hell, it's no need to fucking be in a rush now when I'm already late." I speak out loud to myself as I read the room numbers on the classroom doors like I'm playing bingo of boredom. 19A, 21A; I start off reading the odd numbers on the right side and the even on the opposite side of the hall. Which is where I notice my classroom; 22A.

"Well here goes fucking nothing." I mumble under my breath as I reach for the doorknob, turning it and pulling it up as I make my grand entrance

Chapter Five

Hen's POV

Man, this fucking class is boring as fuck, forreal-forreal. Mutha-fucking niggas in here lying on their fucking dicks, bitches yapping they fucking mouths; sounding like a bunch of fucking cackling ass hens in the fucking hen house. The only reason I'm still in this bitch is because I love the back view of the teacher's ass; when she's writing notes on the chalkboard.

I was just about to lay my head on the desk when I heard the classroom door open and this lil prep-school looking mutha-fucker walks in and looks like he can be the 3rd twin to my unc and pops and they're actual twins. So, I can imagine; right now, everyone thinks we're either brothers or he's my long-lost twin. It's funny because; from the expression on his face and the fact his eyes look like they about to pop the fuck out his fucking head when he notices me; he must be thinking the exact same thing.

By the way he walked in; it was as if he thought he was coming in to make a grand entrance, but that was until he noticed our similarities. I smirk at his ass because he realized just like me; *'Poppa was a rolling stone.'* I sing in my head as dis nigga take the only empty seat right fucking next to me.

I hope his ass ain't looking for me to have any fucking answers because I damn sure ain't got none for him, and I have a few of my own unanswered questions that my pops and uncle better fucking have answers to.

"Excuse me everyone, can I have your attention please? I would like to introduce our new student, Mr. X'avian McTyson". The teacher announces to the class using his government name and causing him to frown because I know he'll rather just go by his street name, I'm assuming.

He stands next to his seat waving like a five-year-old at the THOTs around the class and nods his head to every nigga except for me.

He looks over to me like he has it on his mind while giving me this slick ass fucking smirk at me as he takes his seat again.

'Really my nigga!' I say to myself getting angry at this nigga's attitude like, he bout dat life, I wish da fuck he would! I ain't no punk ass fucking nigga, so I'm let that shit slide just this one time but to show him he ain't on my level, I just huff at

this lil bitch ass while giving him a smirk of my own.

But on a serious tip, this nigga does looks as though he can pass for my dad and uncle damn third twin or either one of them long lost love child. So, I know for a fact he could be related just by looking at him and his last name.

I laugh to myself on that note. "Ahh lil homie, who yo papi?" I whisper at him while trying to annoy the fuck out his ass as an attempt to get under his skin.

"Look bruh! I don't give a fuck who you are right now, but like some people I'm trying to learn." He responds back with a little bit force as he catches me way the fuck off guard because I thought he would be a scary, nerdy ass mother-fucker since his ass walked in here dressed like a prep school nigga with a little swag.

"Excuse da fuck out of me my nigga! But I ain't none of them fuckboys ya use to in yo hood to be catching a bitch fit with me; ya heard me!" I respond back all silly and shit; while rolling my neck like an ole ratchet bitch while making it clear at the end that he doesn't wanna square up with a nigga like me.

The whole damn class starts laughing because of my loud ass mouth and I even got him to laugh as well but he eventually tries to cover it up as he fakes like he was choking on his cough. I extend my fist out to him for some dap but just as I thought; he just leaves it hanging; not even bothering to dap me back which to me is an insult.

"Fuck you then nigga!" I kind of yell at his ass because I'm pissed off at his funky ass attitude, he's been giving me since he walked in this bitch. I guess it's true when they say; you just can't be friendly Bobby with everybody but it's something about this nigga I can't shake.

So, I decide to still introduce myself to him. "Any way in the hood they call me HEN because I'm 'Hit'n Every Nigga' and never spare a bitch life if they fuck with me and mine."

I can't even get mad at him as he tries to hold back from laughing at my street name. I'm used to it though because most people don't get it the first time round and they think I'm calling myself a hen, but later realize I'm far from a chicken ass nigga.

"Mr. Darian McTyson can you and your brother stop interrupting my class please!" Mrs. Hannigen yells at me from behind her desk while using my whole government name and that's why I can't stand her ole funky ass anyway.

"We ain't brothers!" We both say at the same time, then both burst out laughing because we just did a lil twin thing my pops and uncle usually do all the time.

"Oh! Well, umm just be quiet and pay attention!" She responds a bit confused, since we have the same last name. But she decides not to embarrass herself again by standing up and turning to the chalkboard to continue teaching class again like nothing happened.

"Bruh that ass on point!" Lil homie says while nodding his head at Mrs. Hannigen referring to her big ole juicy booty that's shaking and bouncing like a bowl of jello as she writes on the chalkboard.

"I know right, and she got that fiya!" I say using my imitation Jamaican accent.

"You know what I mean." I wink my eye hoping he catches on I'm trying to insinuate, as I lean closer to him; bumping him on the arm with my elbow while trying to whisper so no one else can hear us.

He nods his head while reaching out his fist balled-up, insinuating he wants some dap. I immediately catch on to what he is referring to and without hesitating, I dap him up without any more words being passed for the rest of the class.

Chapter Six

** *Demeekia's POV* **

Man, I hope Nea ass brings my damn project; I left it in her locker for our third block. I'm always first to class since my second block is right across the damn hall, two doors down.

"Good afternoon, Ms. James." the teacher greets me politely as she takes her seat behind her desk.

"Good afternoon! Mrs. Carter." I responded back in my best Smokey imitation as I can muster making her giggle at my response. Finally, the rest of the class start piling in and Hen walks in the class with some lil nigga walking close behind him; looking like his damn twin.

"Wats up, Baby Momma!" He says to me as he takes his seat next to me; he leans over giving me a kiss on the cheek.

I'm not actually his baby momma but I almost was, until I lost our baby when I got into a fight during our Jr year because some bitch wanna claim she was fucking him too; she ain't the first or won't be the last. So, I'm glad this year; I ain't having the same fucking problem this year since. I already made it clear that I'm his Day One Bitch and can't be replaced.

"Hi baby; whose this weak ass imitation of my nigga?" I asked him just under a whisper making ole dude frown up at me; like I give a flying fuck.

"Baby be nice! dis here might be my fam; blood related ya feel meh!" He replied back to me; all calm and shit but sternly at the same time, so I just shrug my shoulders and I decided to drop it for now.

"Wats up lil momma!" He responded, shocking the shit out my ass that he actually sounds all hood and shit but dressed all prep with some swag.

I hear both Hen and Prep Boi; I'm calling him that for now because I don't know his name or street yet. They both continue to laugh hysterically at my ass like it was that funny.

"Shut up fuck ole mark ass!" I semi-yell at their ass for laughing but instead they laugh even harder till I punch the fuck out them both making them rub their arms where I just hit them.

"What's Prep Boi name anyway!" I refer to his street to Hen as he stops short of laughing and looks like he doesn't know as well.

"Ahh, you know what my nigga; I never did ask ya yo street name?" He turns behind him to Prep Boi as he waits for his response.

"Oh! Its Vicious; my nigga." He responds a lil too cocky for my likings but long as Hen don't seem to mind; it ain't my place to check him on it.

I turn my attention now from them as I begin to get impatient while waiting on Nea ass to get here. As always, she comes in just as the bell ring; making her almost late.

"Heyyyy My Bitch!" She whisper yells to me, taking her seat behind me; but next to Vicious. I notice he starts all frowning at her ass, for whatever reason I don't know.

"Mrs. Jenkins, I see you still like to cut it close." Mrs. Carter scolds Nea for the umpteenth time.

"Sorry Mrs. Carter!" She responded back, imitating Smokey's voice from the movie Friday. Mrs. Carter just rolls her damn eyes like always; making the whole class laugh out loud.

"Ok, class we have a new student; Mr. X'avian McTyson." She says, all shocked and confused as me, we then look between Hen and Vicious.

Suddenly, I hear a slight gasp from behind me. I guess after the shock wore off; Nea finally realizes

Vicious' presence next to her but brushes it off like he isn't there. Hmm, I wonder what's the beef between them two; I guess I'll play Sherlock Holms later.

Mrs. Carter then announces to those who had a makeup project to do; to pass it up to the front. I slightly start to panic until Nea leans forward and whispers; "I got you; here's ya shit Bitch!" Then starts to laugh out loud at my ass because I thought she forgot my project and almost panicked. I sighed a breath of relief before passing my paper to the front.

Chapter Seven

** Ayranea's POV**

So, can you believe this Preppy looking mitch has a fucking class with me, and on top that he looks like Hen twin fucking brother.

Man, I didn't even know this nigga had a twin. They almost sound like they didn't either. Not that I'm trying to listen to their convocation or anything, because I can care fucking less. I notice from my side view that the damn nigga drooling hard ova Mrs. Carter though; I can't even get mad cause shit the whole class gawk ova her juicy booty ass.

It's tight, bounces when she moves around the front of the class; oh, weee bruh! Don't get me wrong; I ain't at all gay but shit how she packing.

"I'll hit dat!" Not realizing I must have said out loud; cause now this nigga Xav staring at me with a smirk like he was thinking the same damn thing.

"Bruh I was thinking the same exact thing; you ain't one them fem chicks who likes fems or stud are ya?" He asked with curiosity laced in his tone.

"Hell naw! I'm strictly dickly my nigga!" For a minute I swear I notice a glimpse of relief wash over his face, but it's gone before I can really be for sure. I thought I whispered yell until I heard everyone laughing close around us; even Mrs. Carter who added;

"From time to time!" Making the whole class gasp but me, Hen and Meekia because we had that already but not all at the same time but shit, we talked about it like we did.

** Vicious' POV**

'Man! did I just hear this bitch right, when she said, from time to time; like she likes her kisses down low. Shit! I can make her arch her back and that pussy purr, she ain't been with a nigga like me; is what it sounds like.' I think to myself, then blurted out loud.

"Oh, my fucking gosh! Get out your fucking dildos and best vibrating toys! It's about to get freaky in this bitch!" I yell, imitating a prep school freaky chick. Yo don't sleep on them hoes, they freaky as fuck, and I know from experience.

The whole class burst out laughing except Hen, his ole lady, shawty on side me and Mrs. Carter who all share the same expression of guilt.

"Oh, I know y'all didn't!"

"Boy, shut the fuck up! Ain't nobody did shit!" Shawty said next to me. But how she said it doesn't sound too convincing, but more like a cover up.

"Ok class shows over! Please, copy what's on the board and then we'll discuss it when you're done." Mrs. Carter says, as she gives the class instructions for the work we're supposed to have started before the chaos started with shawty's slick comment. Here I go thinking about her once again. On the real though, she's fine as fuck and I need to inquire around, to see if she snagged or not.

"A nigga on a mission!" I say out loud for her to hear and she does, because now she's looking at me like; I just grew a second fucking head.

"Man! shut da fuck up and pay a-fucking-ttention!" Hen whisper yells, looking annoyed and shit but yeah, he's right schooling come first.

So, finally since I came into class; I try to pay-a-ttention, even if it's hard with all that ass jiggling in the front of the classroom; like a bowl jelly with legs.

Chapter Eight

Hen's POV

So, since our first block; me and Vicious have been trying to connect the dots to see how we may be related. I've been trying to reach my pops and uncle but, I ain't received no answer from either of them yet. So in the meantime I'm just going by what I know and from what he told me; so far about his mom passing away a few months ago; from an armed robbery.

It was all ova the news and I do remember how my unc almost lost it. He is known to be a Ham in the streets, which means he's a 'Heartless Ass Muthafucker' when anybody fuck with someone he loves. He went crazy trying to find out who the mark ass nigga was that took out the chick in a carjacking. Come to find out; it was ova Vicious' mom. So, I've already left him a message telling him what he told me and that we need to talk ASAP. So, he knows it's a possibility this lil nigga could be his son and he didn't even know it, till I texted him.

He finally responds back through text and says that we need to skip lunch time, so he can talk to him; him referring to Vicious.

"So, who's down for skipping lunch?" I say, putting it out there for Nea up tight ass; because her ass may need some persuasion, and well my dude Vicious, he just doesn't have no damn choice, especially if he wants answers. Plus, I already know my baby Meekia's down for skipping class because we do it all the time during lunch.

"Man! I'm hungry, I ain't ate shit this morning. Mom's doing a double, and Asia's going over to Tashie's house after school, but I still have to be home before she gets dropped off tonight. I ain't missing lunch unless you buying." Nea responds and complains about being hungry, and rolling her neck, while she explains the situation of being on time for her sister.

"Man, you're just scary that's all. Tashie's mom can drop her off at the studio where we're going, and I can drop ya'll home." I respond back teasingly, but in a serious tone at the end, as everyone else laughs at our childish behavior.

"Wateva Darian!" She responded back to me in a whining tone because she knows I'm right and she only used my gov name when she's mad at me. Like she is now.

She has been like a lil sis from another mother, since the sandbox in elementary and I dare Meekia to complain. Yeah! She my girl and all but Demeekia didn't join the picture till middle school; I don't give a fuck if she gets mad or not; Nea is Fam.

"You down as well, right?" I directed that question toward Vicious, who seemed a little nervous; since I mentioned to him that we were skipping. I think he's just nervous about the possibility of finally meeting his pops; which would really prove he is my blood fam.

"Yeah, I'm down, I just have to text my uncle that I am going to be late getting home after school." He responded back all cocky like I know him to be so far.

This lil nigga hard to figure out; that could be a good and bad thing in the street. Being unpredictable to me, is on point but he is just a lil too cocky for my likings. But it seems to work in his favor, and I can tell by his cockiness that he can hold his own.

"Nea! you riding with my dawg, right?" She quickly frowned and gave me the stank face, when I asked her that and I already knew she was about to have bitch- fit.

"Yeah! Shawty you can ride in my wipp."
Vicious says to her smiling and shit before she can whine about it.

Shit, from the way he has been checking her out on the slick, you'll swear he's feeling her ass hard, but I'll check him on that on a later date; right now, we all need to get loaded in our shit; so we can ride out forreal-forreal.

"Man! look here; we need to stop pussy footing around so we don't get fucking caught my nigga." I snap at their ass cause now they annoying the fuck out me; especially Nea ass.

"Ight lets go then, shit!"

Vicious says in his usual cocky tone, as Miss Pre-Madonna, begins to whine about riding with him and not us as we all head to the student's parking lot; sometimes she can work a nigga fucking nerves and this is definitely one of those fucking moments. Finally, we make it to our wipp and Nea still has not shut the fuck up.

I head over to the passenger side of my wipp and open the door first for my girl to get in; she plops her fine ass down in the seat and I close the door for her. Just as I head over to the driver side; I notice baby girl standing next to my car as she is waiting for me to open the door for her.

"Naw, you riding with my nigga so, go ahead with him to his wipp!" She then crosses her arms over her chest and stands there like I'm going to change my mind or something; I just brush past her and head to the driver side. I notice she's still standing there, and I just shake my fucking head at her stubbornness.

"Bruh, go get in his car now! Before we leave your ass." I yell, aggravated with her fucking attitude, with a not so idle threat at the end.

"Ahh! Fine; you get on my damn nerves Darian!" She says, sounding defeated and giving me the middle finger, as I point her in Vicious' direction.

"Yeah, love you too." I say, as I notice Vicious standing near his wipp parked not far from mine. Soon as she makes it over there; I shake my head at her ass again for giving him a hard time. Now, I really had enough of her stupid ass.

"Look bruh! Get your stupid ass in the damn car Ayranea, before I come the fuck over there and throw yo bitch ass in his fucking trunk, so fucking pick!" I yell at her ass as I begin to walk in their direction, but stop as I see she quickly plopped her ass down in his car without so much as a mumble after I said that.

I notice my nigga face looks relieved as fuck, then he mouths a quick thank you as he quickly shut her door and jogged around to the back of his car to the driver side.

Before he can hop behind the wheel, I yell at him to follow me. He nods his head but gives me this 'no; dull look', which makes me wanna face-palm my ass for saying the obvious. I give him a nod back as we get our wipp at the same time; finally peeling off before we get caught for skipping.

Chapter Nine

Ten minutes later…

Vicious' POV

   I pull up onside my nigga; wondering why he brought us here and not to his dad or Unc's house. But before I can turn off the car, shawty already bounced her ass out my wipp and slamming my damn door a lil too hard for my liking; but fuck it. I'm on a whole other mission right now. I jumped in my seat when I heard someone tap on the driver side window making me realize how deep I was in my thoughts.

   "Hey, are you just going to sit and stare off in space, my nigga!"

Hen dumbass yells from outside my widow with a stern look on his face. I don't bother saying anything because at this point my nerves have gotten the best of me. I'm nervous as fuck right now. I'm about to come face to face with the man I heard nothing but the worst about, from my grandpa and mom.

I never could understand the real beef my grandpa had against him other than the fact he abandoned my mom when he found out she was pregnant with me. My mom just never wanted to talk about it to me because it seemed like a touchy subject for her every time I brought it up.

"Bruh you alright?" I turn in the direction that I heard Hen's voice and realize he's sitting next to me in the passenger seat with the door close; I didn't even hear him get in.

"I can't pretend to know how you're feeling right now, because I've never been in a situation like this before; so, we can just chill here till you feel up to going in." Hen responds understandably, making me feel thankful he's here now.

"I've heard nothing but negative shit about him through my family and it's like, I'm about to open up Pandora's box; ya feel me and it's about to blow some shit out the water! All I ever heard was one side of the story and was left to believe that; now I get a chance of a lifetime to hear his side, when I should have heard it from my mom. But I can't because she took her side with her to the grave." I say as I continue venting, with a lace of anger at the end towards my mom.

"Did he ever try to reach out to her, or did he just say fuck her?" I asked Hen, as if he would know the answer. He didn't try to answer or say something smart like, why I'm asking him. Which I'm grateful that he was just being understanding right now, because it eased some of my nerves.

"Maybe I should just ball up my feelings and questions so I can get the shit over with; what you think?" I asked Hen, as I shake the rest of my nerves and uneasiness aside.

"I think you need to get your head right; don't go in there with what you know; but instead, go in open minded to what he has to say on his behalf. You can't just walk in and go off assumptions that may or may not even be 100% true; cause outside looking in, it seems as if they were trying to keep you from finding out the truth behind your mom and dad. I just picked that off by what you just said; ya feel me."

"Yeah, you right." I said, feeling back in good spirits after talking with him. *Now my mind feels a lil more at ease, but I'm hungry as fuck though. maybe we should run by BK for something to eat.* I think to myself before saying anything out loud.

"Yo! call the girls out; I'm hungry as fuck and was thinking about going to BK and then, we can handle this shit after." I tell him as I start the car back up. He just nods in response and then opens the door to get the girls.

I see shawty walk out still with an attitude, but she'll be alright after her ass eats something. I unlock the back doors for the girls as Hen takes his place back in the front; I start the car again and back out the parking spot and head to BK. Then, I realize this area looks a little familiar but put it off, as I turn left out the parking lot to our destination.

** Random POV**

Man, bruh I can't believe Kenda Moore died a few months ago and now; I found out she had my seed and didn't tell me.

I missed 18 years of my son's life; if it wasn't for my fucking nephew blowing my phone up; talking about he need some answers because the new transfer student looking like he can be his twin; I was thinking like; why the fuck he asking me if his papi slipped up or not.

But he kept insisting that he was mine; but as soon as he mentioned Kenda's death; he didn't have to say no more.

If you haven't figured it out yet; I'm Laronzo X'avian McTyson and I have a twin brother named

Larenzo McTyson who is my nephew's father. See back in my teen years I was in love with this fine nerd chick named Kenda Moore. She would dress super nerdy, but boy did she have a fucking body and a brilliant mind. Every nigga wanted to hit that, but she was one of the hardest chicks to get.

You couldn't just spit any game at her, because she would cut a nigga down to size in a New York second. She was so fucking untouchable even the jocks got rejected but see me, I love a challenge and she was a dime piece, well worth the fight. It took a nigga damn near our whole junior and senior year to get her out her shell. Finally, at prom night she handed over her V-Card to a nigga and trust-da-fucking-plus; it was well worth the wait.

But me being the nigga I was at the time, I made a bet with the fellahs, that I could get it. I actually hate to say it now because it was da biggest mistake of my life. I fucked-n-ducked her; for a measly $40 bet, which not only did I win and take her V; but I broke her heart and left her with my seed. Just thinking about the shit right now have a nigga all choked up.

I tried to reach out to her before graduation; but her fam kept shutting me out and had her pulled out of school causing her to get her diploma early. Shit, a week after graduation; I found out she moved somewhere on the north side in Booshieville and I just stopped trying. Shit what really could I do; ya feel me.

I took a good girl and fucked over her life; just for some pussy and a $40 bet and I still regret it to this day. Shit, my dick still twitch when I think of that night....

Part 2 –

The Unveiling

Chapter Ten

Still from Random POV

FLASHBACK

"Bruh, I don't give a fuck how hard you talk shit, but I bet you fucking $40 that you can't pop her fucking cherry on prom night." My boy says to me as me, my brother and the fellas are chilling at my house down in the game room in the basement; It's him, Key and Mani.

"You're on, my nigga! That's a bet all y'all ass will wish ya never made; trust the fucking plus!"

Shit, between me and my brother, Ratchet high cheerleaders had no chance or mercy from us because we fucked them all and one or two at the same fucking time; we a beast between the sheets.

So, bagging the stuck-up nerd ain't shit to me; you can tell she wants a nigga dick. Out of all the niggas at school and even my brother couldn't bag her; she handed me a piece of her time during her freshman year, and I been working since in breaking down her walls. Shit, now that we in our senior year I made it official to make her think she was my girl, because I was setting her up for our prom night.

"Man, I need some release; text Angela and tell her to get her ass over here, because she can suck a mean dick! You want in?" My brother Larenzo, but known in the streets as Lo'Key, says to me, referring to our main squeeze Angela who can do wonders with that mouth, while asking our friend if he wants to join.

"Nigga, please! y'all handle that; I am already late for my own pussy date." Pharaoh blurted out, as he passes the blunt over to Mani. Suddenly, Rhianna song that Mani uses for his ringtone on his burner begins to play.

BITCH! bettah have my money…blasts in our ears. We already know what time it is. Finally, he answers before it can start over.

"Hello; speak... oh! Yeah, down third huh...I'm on my way that nigga owe me in the thousands...Ight one."

We already knew; when ya hear that exact ringtone from his phone, and the conversation after, it's about his paper.

"We heard; hit us up later!" Me and my brother say at the same time, doing our twin powers thing.

"Ight my niggas; hallah at y'all; one!" Mani says as he gathers his shit to leave, and dap us both up before heading out the door.

"Bruh, Gella said she's on her way, she just texted me back!" I say to Lo'Key, when I tell him what Gela said in her text.

"Cool! So, you in?" I ask already knowing the answer.

"Shid; hell yeah!" He responds, extra excited.

"Open the side door so she can come in; she just texted again and said she's walking up the side entrance right now."

Lo'Key says as I hurry and run over to the side door leading down to the basement from the outside. Soon as I reach it, I notice her standing outside in a long trench coat and my imagination runs wild, as she waltzes past me.

Angela is well experienced because she's a college student, and a big fucking freak. I think to myself as I go to make sure the doors to the basement are closed and locked upstairs.

As I come down the stairs leading from the house, I see my brother already getting his dick sucked first.

I sit beside them and watch as I pull my dick out for her to suck next and begin stroking it with my hand, while I wait for my turn.

She has her lips firmly around the tip of his dick, while she traces her tongue around the head of it. Soon as she opens her mouth; I reach over and push her head down to the base of his dick, making her gag in the process.

Soon as I let go of her head; she comes up coughing but goes back and works her magic until he busts a load in her mouth. I get super excited once she swallows up the last of his cum.

She licks her lips, when she's done with him and seductively crawls over to me on her hands and knees until she is between my legs.

My dick instantly stands up at attention as she positions her lips over it; she knows I hate it when she teases me; so, I roughly grab a fist full of her hair that causes her to gasp. I quickly shove my dick in her mouth; holding her head down while I thrust my hips up and down, making sure my dick goes deep in her throat when I thrust upward into her mouth. She tries to resist but I tug on her hair to say stop and she does; happy that she got my point; I stop thrusting and let go of her head so she can catch her breath.

My brother finds that shit funny, since he busts out laughing; once she is done catching her breath, she pays us no mind as she goes right into sucking my dick the way I like.

I notice my brother pull her lower body to him and lift one of her legs over the couch, he reaches in the couch and pulls out a condom that we stash in the side of the cushion for moments like this.

I turn my body a little so that one of my legs is on the couch and the other is still hanging off the side so that her body is positioned right for him.

I bring my focus back on her and my dick as she twirls her tongue around it, like it's her favorite flavor lollipop; I hear her moan in the process of my brother entering her semi-tight pussy.

She sucks my dick even better as he pumps his dick in and out her treasure box; she's moaning, he's groaning and I'm enjoying it all.

Her lips and tongue tight around my dick, as I match the motion of my brother's strokes.

I start thrusting my hips up and down again but this time without holding down her head; instead, I just let my hand rest on it as I fuck her in the mouth.

I notice he picks up the pace; knowing all too well, that's his telltale sign to when he's about to bust his load again. She always starts to bob her head even faster, as an attempt to make me cum at the same time. But I bust first, since he is working on his second nut.

While he continues pounding inside her; I continue to hold my dick in her mouth while he works to get his second nut out; because she's a screamer, and she tries her best to get a second one out of me.

She may be a fucking pro at the things she can do; but she can never make me bust twice; I notice she stops in mid stride of going down on my dick and a loud muffled moan escape her mouth while her body tremble between my legs.

I hear his groans get louder as well when he gets closer to busting his second nut and I quickly grab the remote to the TV to turn the volume up over his groans; so, we don't get caught this time. Finally, he pulls out and rips the condom off and shoots cum all over her fat, plum ass until there is no drop left. He isn't as aggressive as me because I would have been slapping her on her ass and doing the most.

She finally gives up trying to get me to cum again, stands up while gathering her things to go in the bathroom; so she can wash up before she leaves, while me and my brother dap each other up and then we both stand up at the same time to pull up our pants.

Angela comes out the bathroom looking satisfied and refreshed as she comes over to us with her coat tied tight and gives us each a kiss on the cheek and leaves out the same door she came through; she always comes undressed; It's easy and faster to access.

"Well, on that note; I'm heading to bed after a hot shower because prom is tomorrow, and you have a bet to keep." My brother says teasingly with a chuckle at the end, when he notices my expression when he mentioned the bet.

"Yeah! Yeah! I know, night-night!" I yawn and stretch out on the couch and instantly fall asleep, soon as my brother turns the light off.

Chapter Eleven

Twelve hours later

Seniors After Party

"So, umm! Kenda you wanna come chill with me upstairs in our room?" I ask her a bit nervous which is odd for me because I'm never shy around a female; maybe I'm just trying too hard to seal the deal.

"It sounds like fun, but I think I should get home." She responds while fidgeting with her corset around her wrist. We only been here 4 hours and 30 min; long enough to eat, take pictures, dance to a few songs, ditch her to chill with Trish and her crew, while me and the boys went upstairs to get the room ready.

"It's only 12am and your dad isn't expecting you home till 2am; so, please stay and have fun with me." I respond fibbing a little about the time; her dad actually threatened to throw me in Juvi if I drop her off later than 1am but I don't give a fuck bout no idle threat; my nigga.

"We'll I am feeling a little uncomfortable here because the girl Trisha bailed on me with her girls, when you and your brother left to roam around." She says a little nervous as she looks around through the crowd for my brother prom date.

I fist bump myself in my head because everything went as planned; we had Trish convince her to come as her escort so her father wouldn't suspect she was going to end up alone with me, but being the dad he is; he still gave me an idled threat once he realized I was in the limo with my brother, then once we were done; I texted Trish to leave her alone by herself at our table, so it'll be easier to convince her to come upstairs. Trish thought it was wrong to play on her emotions over a bet, but after my brother put her in check, she left her two cent out of it and went along with the plan.

"Well, if you feel like; that we can go up to the room my mom got for me and my brother just in case, we got too drunk to drive home." I respond casually as I watch her as she looks as though she's thinking about it, and finally nods her head giving me her unspoken answer.

I wrap my arm around the small of her lower back and guide her to the hotel elevator, away from where they held the party in the ballroom. The lobby is empty and semi quiet, besides music coming from the ballroom. Once we make it to the elevator I press the up button, and we stand off to the side just in case people are on the elevator when the doors open.

We heard it ding and the door open, but no one gets off, so I hold the doors for her to head in first and follow behind her after; then I press the number 4 button for the fourth floor.

"You know I love you right, and I wouldn't force you to do anything you don't want but, you are sure you're ready?" I say to her as we step into the elevator and press the 4th floor button once the elevator doors close; standing next to them while waiting for her response.

"I love you too, and I think that if there was anybody I would wanna do it with; that anybody, would be you." Kenda responds softly giving me the confirmation of how this night is going to end.

I move closer to her, pressing my body against hers as I lift her chin and bring my lips close to hers; our little session is interrupted by the ding of the elevator door opening on our floor.

I grab her hand and lead her down to room 438; I can feel her hand trembling as she squeezed my hand. She really is a beautiful girl; she's smart, talented, and curves to make Beyonce jealous, because she doesn't have a body like hers.

Finally, we make it to the room, and I take the key card out of my pocket to open the door; I swipe it across the key reader and it pops open. Her mouth drops down to the floor because I had set it up to set the mood; oh, I'm definitely getting in those thongs.

I watch her like a hulk as she roams around the room in Aww! Her smile is turning me on and the way her prom dress is hugging her firm ass; if you remember Deelishis from 'Flavor Flav', then you already know her body is on point.

"Hey! do you want a glass of wine or maybe a shot of Vodka from the bar?" I ask as I shut the door after putting the 'Do Not Disturb' sign on the outside knob.

"Wine, please!"

I hear her yell as I go to the bar while she takes a seat in the sitting area of our suite. I go over to the bar as I take out two wine glasses from the wine cabinet, and the bottle of XXIV Karat sparkling Rose wine from North Coast, California for $46.99 that my brother and I ordered off our mom's credit card.

Soon as I pop open the cork; my nose is filled with a fresh and clean attractive aroma of citrus, nectarine of effervescence that leaps out of the bottle with lively fruit flavors. As I pour the bright pink sparkler; it pronounces a ribbon of bubbles and substantially mousy foam around the brim of the glass. But the bottle itself holds a secret I know will make her feel special and give up the panties for the efforts I made.

"Here you go baby, but don't drink it yet, I have something to show you." I place my glass on the table as I head back over to the bar to retrieve the bottle.

"See when you turn on the switch at the bottom of the bottle, it distresses by flashing lights and it creates a flashy fun and memorable moment by illuminating the wine, and 24 karat of real edible gold flakes that gives you this Demi-sec sweetness, as you take a sip of the wine."

She looks at the bottle seeing what I said to be true, and I can tell from the sparkle in her eyes that I just sealed the deal; I smile to myself as I pick up my glass and bring her attention back to me and say a toast..."To a night we both will remember."

Clink!!! The glasses make clinking sounds as we tap our glass together and take our first sip, making her giggle as the bubbles tickle her throat, and for the first time I see how innocent she really is, and I realize…she really is a fucking virgin. Fuck.

"Can I have more? This really tastes great." I hear her ask, pulling me from my thoughts as I look down at her glass and notices it's empty down to the last drop.

"Sure, what the hell, bottom's up!"

I say as I pour her another glass; so after pouring her another glass I go over to the bar, grab a mini shot bottle, and down the contents with no hesitation. *I need to get drunk fast before my conscious kick in;*' I think to myself as I continue to down about three more bottles until I was feeling back to ole self.

"You look dwunk!" She says once she notices me clumsily fall on the couch near her.

"And you swounds dwunk!" I say slurring my voice that I didn't recognize as my own.

"You twou!" I hear her point out, as her words slurring worst as mine; causing us to burst out giggling as we stubble to get closer to each other while realizing how wasted we are.

"I twove you Tarenzo!" She drunkenly says as she slaps both her hands on either side of my face as she give me a sloppy kiss, catching me off guard as I break our kiss to say.

"I twove you twou Cwenda!" I respond sounding as drunk as her as we giggling because of the way we try and say our name.

"If we ever have kids, I want them to have our name but backwards." She says out the blue like she's already seeing a future with us together in her head and oddly I want to see that happen.

It was at that moment that I realized this was more than just a bet; drunk or not; I just confessed how I really felt for her, but I ain't backing out no bet.

I can't do this to her drunk, so I get up to go get a bowl of a sorted fruits and a tray of a sorted cheese from the fridge to feed them to her and myself as an attempt to sober us up. Once I get them, I head back to the sitting area and set back on the couch next to her with the bowl in my lap and tray on the table covered so she doesn't see what it is.

"Mmm, this is so romantic!" She says once she notice the bowl of chocolate cover fruits.

"Open up and close your eyes! I tell her as I hold strawberry near her mouth to eat.

She does as I asked and opens her mouth and closes her eyes; I then placed a piece of cheese from the tray, a seedless grape and half a chocolate dip strawberry in her mouth.

She closes it soon as it touches her tongue. Her lips wrap around my fingers as she sucks on them as I pull them out; "fuck!" I mumble as I feel my dick get hard.

I watch as she moans slightly as the flavors burst in her mouth as she chew the fruit and cheese in her mouth with her mouth closed; I do the same combo just to see why she moaning the way she is and soon as I begin chewing it's unexplainable but good as fuck; I begin to chew slow and close my eyes as well just to savior the taste.

I open my eyes just in time to see her standing up from the couch as she says;

"I'll be right back." She responds while sounding a bit more sober and closes her eyes.

I respond by saying: "ok," as she disappears through the doors leading to the bedroom; I continue snack on the fruits that are now sitting on the table. Wanting something a little more solid, I start eating the cracks with the cheese and notice it's really helping me to sober up some.

I hear the bathroom door open and what I see next causes my dick to get even harder; if that's even possible.

Kenda is standing in the doorway of the room in some grey lace bra and matching thongs. Her breast is sitting up plump, round and perky staring at me to free them from their confinement. She gives me a slow seductive twirl as she turns and shows me her firm, round, beach ball ass protruding over the side of her thongs.

I bit my bottom lip as she seductively walked to me in her silver open toe red bottom stilettos; she reached for her phone and began typing something in. When she stops typing; music fills my ears as she sways her hips to the music; I can't even take my eyes off her body as it moves in sync with the beat.

I quickly pull off my jacket, then pull at my tie; because it was somehow choking me. Her movement seems as though it's hypnotizing me to get up out of my clothes.

I notice she glides closer to me; her body moves so elegantly; almost like a seducing belly dancer.

I can't take the teasing anymore; I actually hate it and I'm about to show her how much I do. Without notice, I sweep her over my shoulders making her squeal in my arms as I walk into the bedroom.

I absentmindedly toss her on the bed; roughly rip her thongs off and spread her legs apart. All this catches her off guard, but she allows me to take control.

I then pull her body to the edge of the bed as I get down on my knees and slowly move close to her treasure box; before she can ask what I'm doing; I drive my tongue as deep as I could possibly go and devour her pussy. I move my tongue around, licking from her clit to her rabbit hole; I spread her folds open wider so I can get better access. Slowly sliding my tongue over her now swollen clit; I get more excited when I hear her moaning out loud.

Chapter Twelve

Continuance Of Seniors After Party

My tongue moves around like a snake in soft but wet grass. I make sure to lick over every inch of her pussy, touching every single nix and cranny. I move my lips closer as I latch them around her swollen erect clit, suckling on it like a baby latching to his mother's breast for the very first time.

I feel her body shake and tremble as I suck on it more; my tongue lap over the tip of it. Her body jerks and trembles more; I love how her body responds to the things; I'm doing to it.

I never got this deep before with anyone; she's my first to do this with, and the way I have her moaning and groaning, while pulling and scratching at the sheets. I know, I'm doing a good job. So, I decide to try something else to get her ready for my rock-hard dick.

I remove one of her legs from my shoulder and push two fingers as deep as I can inside her pussy, and rest them there till she adjusts.

But not once, do I slack up with my tongue; as soon as her body relaxes to my sudden movement from before; I slowly start to pump my fingers in and out her pussy; making her clinch her pussy walls tight around them.

She moans again and tries to buck me away, but I stay latched on and pump my fingers even faster inside her. Again, unsuspectedly I add a third finger and pump it with the other two.

This causes her to buck harder and I'm loving every moment of it; I want her to not to hold back.

I can tell she is, whether she knows it or not. Just for a second, I let go of her clit and she released a huge breath of air; *'Damn! I'm doing that good that she forgot how to breathe.'* I say to myself as I mentally pat myself on the back.

"Don't do that again! Stop holding back; it's ok to let it go!" I scold her for holding her breath, she needs to try breathing through not matter how good it feels.

She tries to respond but her voice is caught up in her throat. "If you can't take it anymore and need me to stop just tap the right side of the bed and I will stop." I explain to her letting a little of my dominant side out and explaining her choice to tap out if it gets too intense for her.

"O-oh OK." She manages to respond as she tries to wrap her mind around the concept of getting her pussy ate; well in this case devoured.

Without saying another word, I go back to working my fingers again inside her but this time I want to watch her expression for a bit; when she begins to moan again; I add another finger in.

She tenses up and relaxes as I change my pace to a slower rhythm; I gradually pick up the pace again getting her ready for my dick. She slowly starts to move with the rhythm of my fingers pumping in and out of her, and I realize she's ready for the real thing.

"Close your eyes and don't open them until you're ready to join in." I instruct her to do as I say, as I get ready to remove my fingers and she does as she was told, I quickly remove my fingers and thrust my dick deep inside her; she notices the difference and whimper softly because of the pain she feels.

"Relax; don't tense up." I instruct her again as I wait for her to relax.

She slowly begins to relax, and I slowly begin to pull back; only leaving the tip in.

"Take a deep breath as I thrust in and exhale as I pull out, until it doesn't hurt anymore." I instruct her one more time before going her my full length; she nods her head and I wait till she takes a deep breath, as I quickly thrust in to void her V card.

I drive it deeper than I did before; and it feels like I just popped a water balloon; which makes it feel even better than before.

For a moment, I forgot she was even a virgin and before I realized it, I was fucking her like I never did anyone before. I started off going a bit fast; because it felt so-fucking-great; how her wall wraps around me like a glove. I lift both her legs over my shoulder, as I begin to pound deeper, but she won't allow me to and it's starting to piss me off; that she's keeping me from going as deep as I want. Doesn't she realizes-how-amazing-this feels?

I decide to slow up my pace because she's resisting too much to fuck her, like I usually would with someone else. So, I change it up to slow and even strokes; and not wild and forceful like I used to.

She seems to like it this way because she's moving her hips to match my pace; no chick has ever done what she's doing and for a minute; I'm taken aback by her movements. It's like our bodies are moving like we're one and I really like it this way.

"I wanna try riding you?" She asked me as I look taken aback by her boldness. I almost don't know how to respond because this is something else that's new to me, I'm excited to give it a try.

I pull out slowly and lay on the bed next to her; she proceeds to straddle my mid-section. This is something new for me. So, I don't know what to do next; she notices and suddenly takes control. She grabs my dick in her hand and raises up a bit to guide it in and slowly slides down on it. She tenses up, when she feels it hit her back walls but then begins to move her hips back and forth.

I moan in pleasure as she works her body, like she knows what she's doing; my hands grip firmly around her ass, as I guide her to bounce up and down.

She follows my lead and suddenly things get wild; she bounces faster, rocks her hips harder, causing her breast to bounce up and down in front of my face as she leans forward.

Again, our bodies move in sync; we're moaning the same, breathing at the same pace and I can't help but feel like our bodies fit right together.

I feel something build inside me; and I know it's not a nut because it doesn't feel the same, but it still feels great!

Her body tenses up the same and we move together faster; she digs her nails in my chest and it doesn't seem to bother me.

I feel now as though I wanna cum; but I still can't, and I can't explain why. She begins to tremble again; but this time she moves her body faster like she can't cum either.

I'm confused because I never lasted this long; then I get an instinct to thrust my hips upwards as she bounces up and down and finally, I feel like I can nut.

She moans something I can't understand; but I'm too focused on releasing all this build up. Suddenly, I feel her squeezing her walls around my dick and I just lose all control, when I feel this warm liquid going down my dick.

It feels so great that I finally explode deep inside her and that's when I realized; I forgot to put a condom on. It dawns on me that this is the first time, I ever penetrated someone's pussy and not their ass; like I usually do.

I shoved her off top me because I'm pissed that I allowed this to get this far. I put it in her pussy, I've never fucked without a condom, what the fuck did I just do? I realized I got too cocky because I hate to be teased, but she was only trying to loosen up to me.

Doing all the rambling in my head; I jump from the bed and begin to get back dress, like I always do after sex.

I guess she thought I was going to leave; but I was only putting on my pants. I sit back on the bed with my hands against my head because I know I just fucked up.

I didn't even notice her panic or realize she thought she was just a fuck; I didn't pay attention to her cries from the bathroom as she rushed and put her clothes back on.

I was so caught up on the realization of the fact that I made love to someone. That I didn't hear her crying while she ran out the bedroom and out the room door. Until it hit me; that you don't make love to someone, unless you love them from the heart.

I was about to ask if she was ok and apologize for how I pushed her off but she was already gone and it made me feel like shit; as I ran out the room to explain it to her but she was already in the elevator.

She didn't come back to school after prom or show up for graduation. Her brother even beat the shit out my ass and I took my licks because I lost her over a stupid fucking bet and not telling her before she left, that she wasn't just a fuck; we made love and it meant everything to me that it was with her.

My first love.

Chapter Thirteen

Back to the present...

So if it wasn't for the news broadcasting about a random arm robbery that caused the death of Chicago's police Commissioners' daughter, Kenda Moore; at a convenient store on the north side of Chi-town; I wouldn't have known she was dead.

That shit right there just blew my fucking mind, especially when her picture popped up on the screen clarifying it was really her; because I don't know how the fuck the street's biggest crook, crawled his way to become a fucking a Commissioner, any damn way.

Shit! That hit a nigga hard bruh; to hear ya first love being announced dead on the scene; over a nigga robbing her at gun point for her damn car, ya feel me!

It made a nigga go HAM; making me a Hit-And-Murda nigga in the streets, just so I could find the mitch who took my heart bruh. It only took a nigga like me, with the history I had in the streets from when I was young and my dad running the

Southside of Chi-town before he died, a week to find him with ease.

Trust when I did, this mark ass nigga saw his life flash before his fucking eyes. I didn't even have to put one fucking finger on his bitch ass before he started pleading for his life, soon as he seen who he was dealing with.

They don't call me 'Ghost' For nothing my nigga. I am the last person you wanna see; before I hand yo ass a first-class ticket to hell. But this one particular nigga; I had something different in mind for his mark ass.

I was doing this for her fam, or so I thought, because somebody tried they best to get him off; but not even money can fuck with solid evidence.

So, after damn near beating this nigga to death I was getting all the information I need except for who hired him; whoever did it had to have top notch power over his ass to not even snitch. I still had enough evidence and had my boys to drop his ass in front CPD hands with a full tape confession about the robbery, the chop shop where he brought her car, and the gun he used to shoot my girl.

The DA tried to get him off until they pulled out the evidence we provided, then he just left his ass for the judge to handle because it was nothing he could do to get him off.

Now he's in jail doing 25 to life while getting his ass served on a silver platter; I paid damn good money to see his ass suffer in that hell hole. Pun intended lol! I did all that because she will always be my Day one that got away. I was trying to tell her that after I found out she was pregnant with my seed; I saw it as an opportunity to make things right, because she changed a nigga whole mind frame.

"Bro you ight?" My brother asks all frantic and shit after he busted in my damn office like the fucking building on fire or something. I suddenly notice my cheeks all wet from crying after reliving Kenda memories and death again in my head.

It's a twin thing; that this nigga always knows when I need to vent and feel when I'm distressed.

"Damn! You're still hurt over Kenda; huh bruh?" He gives me this empathic look mixed with concern.

"Yeah, she's that one that got away bruh; now I can't ever get her back and even though I moved on, I still love her." At this point, I'm too torn to hold back more tears and just let them all out. If a nigga ever said he ain't cry before; get that Muthafucker Committed; he crazy as fuck!

"You know her family even kicked me out the church at her funeral; like it was my fucking fault bruh!" I yell slightly as I start to get angry; over the fact her family is still holding that bullshit over my head.

"Even after all these years bruh; I mean I ain't seen her since our prom night and the day after at school while I got my ass whooped by her fucking brother like I raped her or something." I say as I continue venting about how shit played out after prom.

"They kept me from speaking to her; even after I found out from some chick that was dating her brother; that she was knocked up with my seed!" I yell even louder as I slam my fist against my desk, fucking mad as fuck right now.

"I tried to step up and do the right thing for my seed by trying to reach out to her, ya feel me? I wanted to be there for my first born but her fucking family took that opportunity away from me." I continued to vent out to my brother as I was finally getting all that shit off my chest. I didn't realize I was bawling my eyes out, until my brother was over me while patting my back trying to calm me down.

It wasn't till I looked up after I heard them gasp; that I finally noticed the lil Prep dressed nigga with some swagg; looking like Kenda standing in the doorway with his fist all balled up, like he wanna fuck a nigga up, and my nephew standing behind him his mouth open in shock.

Chapter Fourteen

Vicious' POV

We finally make it back to the studio and now I'm more than eager to get some answers. Soon as we walk in the lobby, we wave to the secretary at the desk and the security guard standing next to it, trying to spit his game at ole gurl. I continue to follow Hen and the girls to the elevator; I notice as the door closes the security guard's confused expression, when he gets a clear view of my face. I must have zoned out again because I'm the only one who hasn't stepped out of the elevator.

We pass up a recording booth with this vanilla nigga trying too hard to rap. The girls stay behind to watch that fucking clown make a fool out his ass; while me and Hen continue down the hall to his Unc's office. We ain't even half way down the hall yet, and I can already hear some nigga yelling, all loud and shit.

You can tell, he's all caught up in his feeling over some serious and emotional shit. But what catches my attention and stops me dead in my tracks, as I stand in front of the second to last door at the end of the hallway, was what he said.

"Yeah, she's the one that got away bruh; now I can't even get her back and even though I moved on, I still love her. You know her family even kicked me out the church at her funeral; like it was my fucking fault bruh! Even after all these years bruh, I mean I ain't seen her since our Prom night and the day after at school I got my ass whooped by her fucking brother like I raped her or something. They kept me from speaking to her, even after I found out from some chick that was dating her brother; that she was knocked up with my seed! I tried to step up and do the right thing for my seed by trying to reach out to her, ya feel me? I wanted to be there for my first born but her fucking family took that opportunity away from me."

By the time he was done venting, he was bawling his eyes out letting out all the pain he was holding in for my mom out.

Then I gasp when realizations hit me; that he was my father and he loved my mom after all these years, and it made them finally notice me in the doorway with HEN, because they're looking from me, to each other; all shocked and shit as I just stand in the doorway with my fist balled up, because I wanna call him out on it; that every fucking word I just heard him say was a lie; right? But from the emotions in his words, I knew he was telling the truth, and my grandpa an my mother told me nothing but lies about my father.

I noticed the dude who's standing up next to him, looking like a carbon copy of the guy who I'm staring at. He looks exactly like the one who I'm sure is my dad. He stares at me with a confused as fuck expression on his face. Taps the one crying over my mom on the shoulder to get his attention, as he looks up first at him, then over to us when his look-alike nods his head in my direction. Making him finally notice me, as realization hits him like a reality check, that I'm his son.

'Woo! That shit really just hit a nigga hard like a ton of bricks. He just confirmed the shit I was told about him was all lies, and he also just confirmed that he's my damn pops.' I think to myself as I start to get a little lightheaded as all the pieces started to connect.

"Man, you alright bruh?" I heard someone in the room ask me, but my head is too fucked up to know who just asked me that; which I'm mostly sure it was HEN, since he's standing the closest to me.

"At this point I'm mad as fuck right now bruh; they fucking lied to me!" I shout out loud under my breath; shocked right now is an understatement to say the least.

"Every fucking one of them son-of-bitches; lied to me!" I yell even louder because by this time all his words are starting to soak in deep.

"My own fucking mother, just took the fact that all my fucking life, I was being lied to; literally to her fucking grave."

"Because she knew, who my fucking father was all this fucking time and never fucking tried to tell me." I yell while pacing back and forth when I'm mad that she really took that shit to the grave with her.

"I know that's my mom and all, but I hope she burns in hell for that shit!" I say incoherently out loud because I'm that fucking pissed off, that I didn't say it in my head like I had thought, because I think I hear my dad say: "watch ya fucking mouth, she still your fucking mom." But I still continued to vent.

"I bet! Nonah-dem mutha-fuckers was planning on telling me the fucking truth!" I yell as I realized my uncle Tate and my grandpa knew about my father's mistake that he made when he was young, and they still trying to hold it over his head; 18yrs later, that he made when he was young, and they are still trying to hold it over his head till this day.

"Man, I was so fucking mad thinking; this nigga has the audacity to fucking try and come to my mom's funeral to finally see her and pay his respects to her, so he clears his guilty conscious. But instead, it was them who kept me away from my own father, all dis fucking time!"

I yell in realization; finally getting everything off my chest as I let my tears fall freely because I can no longer hold back all my emotions just like my father was doing, when I was standing in the doorway of his office earlier.

I feel someone's hand lay comfortably on my shoulder and squeeze it lightly, as an attempt to calm me down. It doesn't take a rocket scientist to know its Hen doing it, whispering to me; the same way his dad was doing to mine a few minutes ago.

Hell! I didn't even know I was crying until I heard my dad's voice from in front of me coaching me to let it all out with his hand on my other shoulder.

"Bro would you and nephew mind if y'all step out, so we could talk?" I hear him whisper to his brother and Hen; but I catch him by the arm just as he is about to leave with his dad. I turn to him and ask just above a whisper; "Can y'all stay with me-bruh; please." I whisper ova my shoulder to them because right now, I only trust who's ever in this room.

Because they've never lied to me and Hen brought my father in my life and stayed, when I needed him the most.

I notice him nod as his father shut the door to give us some privacy and then we all head over to the chairs and couch to sit and talk.

Chapter Fifteen

Laronzo's POV

I already can see that him and my nephew Hen are going to be close as fuck because of his actions. I guess, right now Hen and everyone else in the room are the only ones he can trust, and I don't blame him; since everyone else lied to him for the past 18 years.

Hell! he looks the spitting image of me; more than my damn twin, shit. But looking at Hen and my brother; he looks the same way to his dad more than me. I guess it's a twin gene thing, for our kids to look similar to being twins to each other as much as their twin fathers.

We're all sitting on the couch in an awkward silence facing each other, not sure who should speak first. Me and Lo'Key is sitting in the chairs on side each other, while my son and Hen sit on the couch next to each across from us.

"Bruh! This shit like a Déjà vu moment because just a few minutes ago; that was just like me and you." My brother whispered to me; snapping me out my daze; making me realize, I was just staring at my son; pin-pointing our similarities.

"I know right bruh." I whisper back to him, while laughing to myself at the end.

"So, I guess you're my pops, right? And he's your identical twin." I heard my son asking me the obvious questions; a lil choked up still.

"Yeah, that would be me he is your uncle Renzo because his name is Larenzo." I respond back, introducing by his nickname and government name.

"What's up!" My brother replies a lil hesitant, with a salty tone because I introduce him by his government and not his street name, like I know he would have preferred.

I don't need a DNA test to prove he is my seed because; he's a spitting image of me with his momma's hazelnut eyes.

"What's yo name lil homie?

We asked at the same time; it's another thing we do as twins; say what the other is thinking before we can say it ourselves or say it at the same time as we just did.

When I glance at him; I notice he is now sitting straight up like a lil G before he responds:

"It's X'avian Laronzo McTyson-Moore but in school I'm registered as a McTyson."

He says sounding all proud that everyone knows him by McTyson and not Moore at school; I guess his uncle didn't want him to have unwanted attention his mom's death and his grandpa's position as CPD commissioner. But I have a gut feeling it was because he knew my nephew and him would eventually meet and connect the dots because of their last names.

After a minute, I realize that his mom sort of named him after me but backwards, and I can't help but radiate with pride that she at least gave him something of me and kept the promise we made, the one only time I was trying to get to know her.

At the time, I thought it was a joke, that if we ever had kids; we would name them almost after ourselves but using our name vice versa with our middle-names as their first and first-names as their middle; I guess she wasn't as drunk as I thought when she said that. She could've done it as a reminder of me, or she could have done it as a sure way for me to identify him as my son, if we ever crossed paths like now.

"Damn Bruh! He has your whole name; but backwards instead." Lo'Key blurts out loud with shocked tone, as he beat me to the punch before I can say the exact shit I was thinking to myself in my head.

I glance over at my son, who looks clueless as fuck because he ain't caught on yet that he's named after me. That's one of his mom's traits that I loved most about her; she was so green to the street life, that I'm surprised he has a lil hood swagg to his prep boy persona in his ass.

You can tell though; just by how he talks and acts like he has been around some real ole G's. But I don't see how, because his whole mom's side of the family is booshie as fuck except for his crooked ass grandpa; so, it might just run in his blood.

We all burst out laughing, when it finally dawns on him that my name is Laronzo X'avian McTyson.

I think, in her own way she was telling him who his father was by his name; even though she didn't get the chance to explain it to him before she died, and she never seemed like a person to keep a secret this deep to herself; I think she was murdered because she was planning on telling him.

Chapter Sixteen

Unknown POV

I'm only trying to do my best to give my nephew the opportunity to meet his dad; I moved right up the street from his dad's Studio he owns; about 30 minutes away.

I know for sure his nephew should be around Xavi's age and by chance attending the same school. So, it's no doubt that the friends he's claiming he's hanging out with; is definitely his cousins.

Before I left for college; I always kept him with me, taking him to the park, using him to get girls, and letting him listen to the hottest rap artist out there. I tried spending as much time with him as I could when I would come home to visit from college and made sure he had some swagg; ya feel me. I wanted to have a life of my own and by my junior year while playing basketball; I became MVP and went Pro in my senior year.

I was so fucking siked, that a talent scout from my favorite team; the Boston Celtics; wanted to sign me as soon they saw me play my first senior game.

I was blessed to play a year in a half with them; until one day I decided to come home for my favorite holiday; Thanksgiving or as I like to call it 'Cornbread dressing day' because that's all I like to eat. For me, cornbread dressing is the main course while everything else is just sides; but any who.

I was at one of the courts that I owned and invested into as a way to give back to the community. When some nigga got jealous that I beat him in a fucking game of 21 and shot me in my left knee; ending my whole fucking career.

My dad showed no remorse and I swear he had something to do with me getting shot. No! scratch that; I know! he had something to do with it, but I never could find any evidence or proof since he is a master of keeping his hands clean.

Now, I coach a local basketball team and own a bunch of rec centers. I built and named Moore To Give Community Recreation Center on the whole south side of Chi-town; where I was born and raised.

I wanted to help struggling families who worked deadbeat jobs, juggling three jobs at a time; just to make ends meet, single moms; struggling off a first check because she's a drop out and don't have any experience to work; while raising her son or daughter but still try as best as she can to provide for her kids.

For parents, who have little to no family support and still struggle behind closed doors because they are too prideful to really ask for help; no matter what kind of family problem they have; I help put their kids in college and so they can accomplish their dreams.

I just wanted them to have a chance to be somebody; so, those who sign up at any of my gyms can get into a four-year scholarship; if they don't get accepted into their school of choice.

So, when I heard about my sister's murder; I dropped everything to be there for him because I knew with his mom gone, he was going make it a mission of his own to find his pops and I know off top my pops wasn't going have that and he was going next real soon if I didn't step in.

But, back to what I was saying, thanks to my dad and two hours of looking; we found him curled up in his mom's bed crying; I took custody of him to protect him from being next or getting too rebellious because I can tell he ain't been the same since her death.

I had him transferred from the Prep school she had him, into the same public school we graduated from and where his dad attended as well.

I have a bad feeling about Xav wanting to stay after school to; so, say hanging out with some friends he made; all the sudden. He never would have done that shit at the Prep Academy his mom threw him in. I love that lil nigga like my own but I ain't his daddy and I shouldn't have to step in as one.

I'm his only fucking uncle and it's supposed to be the only role I should've had in his life; he was 10 months when he started talking. So, I wasn't surprised when he called me "Dada" but, I corrected him right off the back. Instead, I taught him to call me Unc and once he got that down, then I taught him how to play his cards. Around me he would speak clear and ghetto as fuck like me, and around his mom and grandparents he acted babyfided/booshie as fuck like I would do around them.

I tried to convince them that they needed to tell him about his father; when he was old enough to understand why he called me Unc once he hit middle school going into junior high; he got mad rebellious. He started to notice all his friends from school being dropped off at school by their pops or father figure; all he had was me and my dad to guide him as best as we could.

You could see it in his eyes that it wasn't enough and nobody wanted to listen to me. I tried to convince my sister to stop listening to our dumbass parents; especially from our dad.

Xav needed to know the truth about his name and father; I never understood why she named him similar to his father's name; if she wasn't going tell him the history of his name.

That's why I moved him in this area, because I knew at one point, they would cross paths; but I was hoping he would hear it from me first because if he finds out on his own, which I have this gut feeling he already has, it wouldn't be good.

Man, that's a fucking can of worms; we all going fucking wish stayed closed; I know he's going to hate us for lying and keeping him from his pop.

But, bruh no lie; I just fucking got stuck with a selfish and booshie ass family. That's why, I took him under my wing; so, he wouldn't end like them.

I could've told him about his pops but that wasn't my place and that's why, I'm trying to do what's right and give him the chance to have his father in his life; if anything should happen to me.

It's not like, he ain't never seen the nigga before; he may not remember because at the time, he was like one or two; I had him at the b-court and this nigga was there with his twin.

I couldn't tell them apart from one from the other, even if my life depended on it but one of them seen me trying to scoop Xav up to take him home and went crazy and was about to put one in my dome; because he was thought, I was trying to kidnap his son who was actually my nephew.

If it was for his baby momma, running to the court with his real son; like we had planned, a week before for this to happen; minus his reaction and it was no coincidence that he was dressed like my nephew. I would've been dead, but my nephew would have finally been with his father.

I feel bad for him though because now Ghost knows Kenda had a son for him, and he didn't recognize it was Xav till after the fight broke out and I was already out; he chased after me as I ran to the parking lot. But before he could ask me any questions; I was already gone; I still remember it like it was yesterday.

Chapter Seventeen

Flashback

Yo! Kenda, you mind if I take my little nephew with me to the b-court?" I ask while trying to sound all booshie like her. Ahhhh! This booshie shit makes me wanna throw up.

"Sure, go ahead Lavon Tate!" Kenda yells from the kitchen as I walk through the front door of her townhouse.

I hate when she uses my fucking government; I wanna slap-the-fuck-out-her-booshie-fucking-ass; bruh! Because she was never like this around Xav daddy back in high. Trust me, that bitch can get hood but after what Laronzo did to her after prom; she ain't never been the same since.

Especially, since my dad brain-washed her, making her think his dad was going to be a dead beat. I pleaded and begged for weeks for my dad to at least speak to her. He just wouldn't let up and finally moved us to Booshieville, once they made him commissioner at the North side police department.

Finally, she finished getting him dressed; I squat down with my arms open to pick him up; once I see my nephew running into my open arms as soon as he sees me waiting in the living room.

"Hey, uncle baby!" I say to him once I see him on the floor of the living floor, he runs to his room to get dressed in the outfit I brought for him to put on. I couldn't stay; so, I dropped off for him a few hours earlier; I told Kendra I was taking him to Prat's daughter's birthday party in the park and told her to lay it out on his bed when I came back to pick him up.

"I rweady! Duncle," He responds all babyfided and shit. I pick him up on my arms after giving him a big bear hug; that had him squealing and giggling in my arms as I stood up to leave.

I'm glad that my sis kept him swagged up while I was in college and had him dressed in this all red Jordan jumpsuit with matching 'J's' I dropped off earlier.

"Bye! momma's baby; have fun with uncle ok!" My sister coo to him while I hold him on my shoulder; like I always do when I bring him with me.

"Ok! Sis, I'll bring him back round 5." I tell her as I lean down to kiss her short-ass on the cheek. I sigh a big fucking relief as I walk out the front door; because I can finally drop the prep act.

"You good my nigga!" I ask my nephew as I take him down from my shoulders; so I can strap him in his car seat.

"Yeah, I'm good unc." he replies speaking clearly and shit, like I taught him when he was young.

"Hey! Unc; you coming or you just going to stare off in space?" He asks getting my attention as I got stuck in my head, while going over the plan I setup last week.

Ok! now he's acting too grown for his age; as he yells in my face pulling me out my daze.

"Sorry! My nigga; damn!"

I tell him after securing him in his car seat; I slammed his door shut and jogged around to the driver side. I slammed his door shut and jogged around to the driver side. I quickly open the door, get myself settle in the seat while pushing the key in the ignition and closes the door while throwing it in gear; so we can finally get the fuck out of Booshieville.

So, as soon as I pull up to the court; I notice the last two people I needed to see right now, but the main key components for this plan to work; 'Ghost and Lo'Key;' the McTyson twins.

"Fuck!" I say under my breath.

"Unc, what's wrong with you; nigga?" My nephew asks as I parked and turned off the car while trying to be nosy to see who they were, but his view was blocked by the car beside me.

"Nothing you need to worry about, nephew; come on, let's go shoot some hoops!" I respond to him as I open my door to get out and head around to the passenger side to open his door after I close mine and shove the keys in my pocket.

Soon as I swings open his door; I bend down to unstrap him and noticed he's already has unbuckled himself from his car seat; he rushes out the car as soon as I stand to move out the way to let him out with my ball tight in his hand. He runs full speed to the court, where some other kids his age and a lil older are playing.

"Yo, what's up Triggah!" I hear nigga Prat, yell over to me as I turn from my car as I shut the door and making sure it's locked behind me before I walk over to him and dap him up while keeping a close eye on my nephew.

I see him trying to shoot hoops as short as he is; like, he knows what he's doing with the bigger kids; that doesn't seem okay that he's trying to shoot with them.

"I see you, got yo shadow wit you today, huh bruh!" Prat says after he had to step out the way as my nephew damn near runs into him.

"Yeah! Bruh, he needed a break from Booshieville." I respond, making him crack up on my corny ass joke about the north side.

We both bust out laughing as we continue walking to an empty court.

Prat is like a big brother; from another mother, since my biological dad only had me and he's 7yrs older than me.

But I feel as though I had to take him under my wings because it was something about him that make me feel close to him and not in a gay way, but instead brotherly.

"You ready to make this money?" Prat says as we head to an empty half court.

"Shid! You-know it!" I respond, amped up as I remember my nephew has the ball.

"Let me go get the ball!" I respond as I quickly jog over to where Xav is shooting hoops using some other kids' ball; while mine sit on the side, under the goal where he left it.

'Xav, you good lil man?" I ask him as I bend down to pick up my ball, that he left lying under the goal.

"Yeah, unc I'm good." He responds as he heads back to his game. I shake my head, while giggling at how he acts all grown and shid!

You'll think he's twelve instead of two and a half years old from the way he talks around me; I taught him well.

"Ok! my niggas, let's get-this-shit on the roll; who's up for a game of 21?" I yell to no one in particular.

"The first one to 21 get $100 buck a game till five O'clock." I make sure to yell loud enough for everyone around me to hear, as I bounce the ball over to Prat; waiting for me on the empty court where I left him.

"You on my nigga, that's going to be the easiest $500 I make. Plus, I'll add $50 on every dunk you can make."

I think either Ghost or Lo'Key yelled out from the other side of the court; all cocky and shit with his brother and their crew following behind them as they headed our way.

"Nigga, you on." I respond back; accepting their challenge as I smirk because, I know we have this in the bag.

Me, Prat and the twins stand at the half court line as their crew stand around and watch; I toss the ball in the air and I'm the first one to catch it. I try to rush over to our goal as the twins try to block and steal the ball.

I see an opening and quickly pass it to Prat, who is standing near our goal; he catches it and makes our first shot.

This continue going back and forth for several hours and games; shot for shot, dunk after dunk; it's fucking epic!

I was temporarily lost in thoughts when one of the twins stole the ball from me and made a dunk.

"Nigga! get your fucking head in the fucking game, Bruh forreal-forreal!"

"OK! OK!" Prat hates to lose money with a passion. I look around the court and notice everyone breathing heavy as I try to find a gap to pass the ball over to Prat; but the twins ain't leaving no slack.

Last min, I decide to go for the longest three point shot I ever tried to make; one of the twins catches on to my decision and runs to the goal just in case; I miss the shot.

I get ready, Prat has my back as he tries to block his man from messing up my shot.

"Game Point!" I yell as I get in my stance, aim for the goal and let it rip; I stand there unsure if it's actually going to make it.

Thing one tries to block it; but misses; it looks like it's going in; suddenly it hits the backboard, goes around the rim and finally goes in.

I'm excited-as-fuck-right-now and so is Prat; "We Won! Yayyyy! My nigga; that was the shit!"

"I know right but bruh; them niggas gave us a run for our money." I respond as we all meet half way to collect our winnings.

Chapter Eighteen

We played 10 games; I gave them $1000 which is a $500 split between the twins; they gave us a $1000 as well to split for the games we won a piece; basically we both won five games and on top of that; we made $850 for every dunk me and Prat made on they ass; which were a total of 17 dunks but, I had split that as well with Prat.

Then I still had to turn around pay both them niggas $400 a piece. So, in reality; we came out on top by one fucking shot.

"Nigga! you were off-yo-fucking-game today bruh; what were you thinking about earlier?"

Prat asked as he bring up when thing one stole the ball from me; I don't really have an answer for me getting distracted; so I just shrug my shoulders in response.

"Well, you can pay me for my lost my nigga!" Prat says in serious tone as he refers to the shots the twins made while I was in my head.

"What? Naw, you tripping my nigga!" I respond back but the look on his face tell me he serious as fuck; like I said this nigga don't play about his paper.

So instead of arguing to him about it; I hand him $150 of what I earn; which he doesn't hesitate to take.

After collecting all our money, thing one and two and their crew head over to the benches to catch a breather; while me and Prat head over to get my nephew because it's now 4:45 and if I'm late, I gotta hear his momma's dick-beaters for bringing him home late.

"Nephew! it's time to go my-nigga." I yell half way across the court as Prat follow behind me. He begin to whine and complain as he make his way over to me; as I bounce the ball back and forth between Prat and I.

As I go to grab his hand, once he made it over to me, I'm suddenly pushed forcefully away from him. That shit happened so fast, I barely had time to react.

"Man! Get yo fucking hands off my son; my nigga!" One of the twins yells in my face while trying to pull my nephew from me, as my plan starts to fall in place.

I don't know which of the thing-twins this is, but it has to be Lo'Key because he has a son as well.

"Man! That's my fucking nephew; what-the-fuck you talking about, my nigga!" I yell back in his face as my nephew starts crying because he is scared.

"Let-me-go! I want my uncle; leave-him-alone!" Xav, yells as he tries to get away from him.

"Go to yo uncle then shit, while I handle this lil nigga!" Lo'Key yells at him as he lets go of his hand while thinking he's about to run to Ghost; but instead, he runs behind me.

"What-da-fuck!" Lo'Key yells as he looks at him a bit dumbfounded because he wasn't expecting him to me run behind me, instead of going to Ghost, who is shooting hoops still with their crew.

"Lil-nigga-get-the-fuck-away from him and get-the-fuck-over here!" He screams again at my nephew as it still haven't registered that he isn't his son, as he tries to reach for him again but this time I step in the way; making him confused and pissed at my action.

"My-nigga! You-dumb-as-fuck forreal-forreal! If you ain't figured it out, THAT HE AIN'T YO FUCKING-SON; HE'S MY FUCKING-NEPHEW! MY-FUCKING- NIGGA!"

I repeat myself again trying to get it to register, but the motherfucker so blinded by the fact that Xav looks so much like his son that his dumbass ain't getting what I'm saying, and making me pissed off because he thinks I'm trying to kidnap his son.

Finally, it seems like it's starting to sink in by the way he stares at me dumbfounded, but nods his head when realization hits him that my nephew is his nephew, and not his son, but decided to go along I guess till his brother comes.

Where the fuck is Ghost; he's supposed to be here not him, because out of nowhere, he pulls out his 9mm Glock from behind his back and points the barrow in my face.

'What the fuck, is this nigga bipolar or something? I Thought he was going to play along since he figured it out.' I think to myself as I begin to panic, and finally noticed the crowd of people gathered around, making it click that shit bout to get real ugly real quick.; we got to keep playing it out till Ghost bring his ass here.

"He got a gun!" I hear someone from the crowd yell; I try not to make any sudden moves, as I kneel down beside my nephew; who is now crying hysterically, because he's scared of the situation we're in.

I know Prat has my back; as he makes sure Lo'Key doesn't do something stupid while I talk to my nephew; so, I focus back on him because he's more important right now.

"X'avian, listen to me; take my keys to the car and run as fast as you can." I whisper low enough only for him to hear; as I slowly reach my hand in my side pocket to grab my keys, while trying not to draw attention to what I'm doing.

"Lock-yo-self in it, hide in the front seat; on the floor, call yo mom and tell her that she needs to come get you from the court in our old neighborhood, ok?" I whisper again to him as I put my keys in his small hands.

He begins to cry harder as he holds onto my keys tight in his hands so no one can see them.

"Don't worry about me! Right-now-I-just-need-you-to-do what the fuck I just told you, ok!" I tell him as I firmly squeeze his hand while looking around as Lo'Key stares at him with remorse laced in his eyes, with the gun still pointed at my head.

Xav finally understands my gesture as he sobers up just a lil, when he hears the seriousness of my voice and nods his head in understanding.

"Run as fast as you can and don't look back; Ok! When I sand up; you hurry up and go as soon as I say 3!" I say to him as I begin to count loud enough for him to hear as I slowly proceed to stand up. This is all my fucking sister's and father's fault that I'm even in this fucking situation.

"1, 2, 3!" I notice he takes out running toward the parking; doing as I instructed him to do.

'This is all my fucking sister's and father's fault that I'm even in this fucking situation.' I think as I almost miss that Lo'Key dropped his attention from me and instantly stares in the direction he noticed my nephew ran. And Ghost, who was now standing there, looking like he just seen a ghost, as he looks as though he's about to run after my nephew.

So, I quickly jab Lo'Key ass in the jaw; he drops to the ground and stumbles back to his feet while holding his jaw in shock.

He tried to go for his gun that fell out of his hand; when he hit the ground, but I quickly kicked it away out of his reach.

I then quickly throw another punch in the same jaw as many times as I can; before he can throw his first punch, in hopes that he forgets about my nephew being his son.

He starts to finally grab control of the situation and starts to fight back. We both throw punch-after-punch and blow-for-blow as we fight heads up; just me and him. That was until someone catches me off-guard and I get side-hooked in the left side of my head; making me lose balance and hit the ground.

'I know I said I will do whatever it takes to protect my nephew; even means taking a few 'L's and maybe a bullet or two but this has gone way past what I planned.' I think to myself as I stumble back to my feet; when suddenly I feel sharp pain in my side like someone just kicked me on my right, then another kick on the left side causing a loud crack in my ribs area.

As I stumble to get back up; I feel a sharp pain in my side like someone just kicked me in my right side then I feel another kick on the left side causing a loud crack in my ribs area.

I see someone foot coming straight for my head and quickly roll over on my right side quickly to dodge the impact to avoid being knocked out.

I notice Prat is fighting with Lo'Key while Ghost continues to kick me while I'm down; at this point I'm in too much pain to get up and fight back. *'It's obvious Lo'Key realized that my nephew isn't his son, and a possibility Ghost realized my nephew may be his son, but I don't know if he saw his face or not. This whole fight might be for nothing because Kenda hadn't even brought her ass to the court yet. Which may mean one or two things; my nephew was too scared to call her, or my sister don't remember the b'court I'm talking about to come to.'* I think as I lay balled up getting my ass beat.

So imagine how happy I was when I head a female voice; not belonging to Kenda but who helped me form up this whole plan.

"Baby! -Please-stop! Darian-is-right-here-baby; he's-ok-baby!"

A female screams while running toward the fight; holding who I assume is Lo'Key actual son; who looks like my nephew just a year older.

Now, I see why he thinks; I was trying to take his son because they look so much alike and dressed similarly as planned.

But these nigga ain't paying-no-attention to her and Lo'Key is so amped that the nigga-pushes-her-out-the-way as she tries to block his view from me. I didn't even notice I was fighting him now instead of Ghost until he made her stumble a bit with her son in her arms.

'What these niggas think this is tag-team wrestling?' I think to myself as he manages to punch me in my fucking jaw while I try to regain my focus and to get back on my feet.

125

I quickly swing my arm around and catch him in his left temple with my fist causing him to stumble back.

I hit-him-again; as hard as I could, before he could regain his composure; then, quickly punch him a few times in his ribs. His girl pushes me away from him but he shoves her again out the way, this time causing her to fall as she tries to shield her son from the impact.

I tried to go see if she is okay; but Lo'Key is blocking my view. I use that moment to catch my breath and to avoid his blows.

"Please! You're scaring him; please stop!" She yells as she sits on the ground where she fell, trying to calm her son down, while holding him in her arms.

I feel bad for her and his son now; suddenly, I notice right off the dump that something ain't right about her; she sets her son down on the ground and calls someone to get him; then she reaches for something next to her.

Soon as he is in the clear, she raises her arm in the air with his gun firmly in her hand and pulls the trigger.

POW!!!

Everyone stops fighting and the crowd around us burst out running and finally getting both the twins attention, as they stand in shock as well as the few that stayed around to see how this all will play out.

"DAMMIT! -RENZO, I-FUCKING-SAID-STOP!" She yells at Lo'Key as she turns and points the gun at the twins, but mainly at Ghost, getting his and everyone else's attention, including mine.

'Damn, she a ROD or in other words; she a Ride-Or-Die-chick.' I think to myself as I stare at her with admiration until I hear her clear her throat, breaking me from my trance as she nods her head towards the parking-lot; as a signal for me to leave.

"Shid! She doesn't have to fucking-tell-me twice!" I mumble under my breath as I quickly shoot-out with Prat hot on my trail; as we're running toward the parking-lot; I realized that I left my basketball behind, but at least I'm leaving with my life.

I frantically knock on the window as an attempt to get my nephew's attention; as I notice Prat getting in his car.

He hurries to unlock the door once he sees that it's me; I grab the keys off the seat; where he left them. I quickly put them in the ignition and throw it in reverse; then peel out the parking lot.

I see Ghost running in my direction; through the rear-view mirror. I feel relieved that he finally figured out that my nephew is his son but feel disappointed that he didn't get a chance to officially see his face because of all the commotion.

I guess our plan worked and he now knows; Kenda didn't have an abortion like my dad wanted her to and she had a son. But he still won't get the chance to meet him because; my dad will only make sure of it.

I never went back to that end of the south park since, and gave sole ownership of my gym on that side of town to Prat; so I wouldn't run into them niggas again.

My dad even threatened that if I didn't stop trying to cause trouble on the south side as the police Commissioner's trouble-making-son, and if I didn't stay away from my own nephew; he would have to deal with my behavior, so I wouldn't cause any more trouble. So, I left and moved an hour away from Chi-town and my father.

I let Prat manage the rest of the gyms I owned because I wasn't planning on coming back home. But once I heard on the news of my sister's death, and that he was getting wreck less, I had to come back to protect my nephew and find a way for him to find out the truth about his father on his own.

Chapter Nineteen

Larenzo's POV

'Man! This lil nigga looks so familiar and it ain't because he looks just like my son. Naw, I saw him from somewhere else before, but he wasn't this old.' I think to myself as I try to remember where I saw him.

"Ahh! lil homie; what you said yo uncle name was again?" I ask him because I can't shake the feeling that I met or saw him before......

"Umm! LavonTate." He responds by breaking himself from his lil-chit-chat that he was having with his pops. That name don't ring a bell; but I have heard it, from-some-fucking-where.

"Oh!-Yeah, now-I-remember; he was-that-nigga, I got in a fight with at the b-court back-in-the-day because I thought he was trying to take my son but turned out to be his nephew"! I blurt out loud making everyone in the room look at me all crazy because that just came out random.

"Bruh! You remember that was the same day you fucking realized that he was yours and

Kenda's love child. That nigga; Triggah is Tate aka LavonTate; Kenda's brother, who wooped your ass the next day after prom at school." I yell almost in my brother's face as I hit his arm, trying to make him remember.

"Wait! He was the lil-nigga you were fighting him over?" He says as he points and scrunches up his face up in his son direction while trying to compare the resemblance.

I was doing the actual same shit; until, it hit us; that this lil nigga sitting across from us is the same and my brother doing the twin thing, yells out at the same damn time.

"The-same-lil-nigga; just older now!"

They both look at us confused until they look back and forth from each other realizing how people can mistake them for twins and bust out laughing.

"Mrs. Hannigen, thought the same damn thing in class; only she was half right because we are not brothers." Hen said first as Xav finished his sentence at the end.

"We cousins!" They both say at the same time like; this shit just crazy as fuck that they fucking do the same shit as us.

"Exactly the same shit I was thinking!" My brother say out loud because, we fucking think alike.

Knock!!! Knock!!

Our conversation is briefly interrupted by someone knocking on the door.

"Come in!" I yelled to whoever knocked on the door. Suddenly, it opens and Meekia pokes her head in through the crack then she pushes it all the way open.

"Umm! Sorry to interrupt but Hen can I speak to you outside; please." She asks shyly. Man, I hope he don't fuck up with her because you can tell she's his ROD; like his momma is to me.

"Yeah, I'll be right back, pops. Yo! Vicious, you cool to stay here by yo-self with yo-pops and unc, while I step out to talk to my-shawty; bruh?" He asked him as he responds back cockily. "Bruh really! I asked y'all to stay to make me feel more comfortable in the first place; that's a dumbass question." He snaps back, making him mentally wanna smack himself when he made a valid point making both me and his unc laugh at his ass.

"Bruh you lucky your cocky ass my fam Vicious or else I'll see if yo ass can live up to that name;

my nigga." He just nod his head in response to his statement as he continues his convo with his pops.

'But why the fuck he called him Vicious?' I wonder, confused as fuck until I hear HEN whisper in my ear.

"Dats his street name, pops." before he gets up from the couch; leaving me looking dumbfounded because I didn't catch on quick enough while my brother laughs hysterically because he caught me slipping.

"Nigga! don't feel bad you let yo age slip!" He says while laughing even harder.

"Nigga! You don't want these ole ass hands!" I say jokingly, as I punch him in his arm making him square up as we began to play fight as his son crack-the-fuck at out childish behavior.

Demeekia's POV

"Soooo! What's going on in there; it's been like an hour already and a bitch hungry!" I whisper yell at Hen as he closes the door behind him.

"Bruh! come to find out that's my unc Ghost son up-in-there, and the reason why he looks like my twin with my last name." He whispers yell back to us making both me and Nea gasp like a fish out of water.

"So? Really, he is yo-blood; is your unc going to get DNA to prove it?" I asked and I realize how dumb my question was when I hear Nea ass, bust out laughing.

"Bruh, he don't even need a test; shit the nigga look like all three of us put together." He responded in a dull tone referring to him, his pops and uncle as us. I punched him as hard as I could in the arms for making feel even more stupid for asking a stupid question.

"Shut-up-nigga! Shid, I can have a fucking blonde moment if I want;" I hit his ass again in the same arm that I hit him in before; causing him to laugh even harder.

"Keep-fucking-laughing and see if you can go without this nookie-for-a-fucking week?" He instantly sober up and clear his throat; "sorry baby."

'The power of the pussy; wins again!' I think as HEN stands all apologetic before pulling me in his arms and start kisses me in all my sweet spots until Nea interrupts our makeup moment.

"Man, can we go get something to eat because I'm fucking hungry." Nea hungry ass whine as she stands with her arms crossed over her chest; but I don't mine because I agree.

"Ok-Ok! Damn; I'll call PizzaHut, since we have an open account with them!" HEN groans out loud before walking back in the office; I guess to get permission or something.

"Lets-go back to the studio booth and fuck around on some tracks." I say to Nea as I drag her down to the booth where we first noticed, some vanilla nigga already in there; fucking everyone ears, while he tries to rap.

"Yo! lil mommas, come in here; we might need y'all help". The vanilla, yell to us through the loud speaker.

We squeal like two thirsty bitches; which we're not but shid, we might be on a nigga track; singing hooks and trust me his shit needs the help.

We both flip back our hair dramatically as we walk in super confident; this ain't our first rodeo doing hooks.

This one guy looks sort of familiar; but it's not like I know him or anything, he just looks like someone I-know but don't know. Maybe I know of him through somebody else, he could be a regular or something I seen in here before with someone else, but who-ever-he is; he has a face that reminds me of someone I know; I just can't place where I seen or know him from but fuck it for now.

"So, what's yo name shawty?" He says directing his attention to Nea because everyone in Chicago knows; I'm HEN's D1.

"It's Ayranea!" She responds back nonchalantly with lil hint of "Back-the-Fuck-off-look"; making it clear to him, that-she-ain't-interested!

"Oh! My; bad-shawty! I didn't know-you, one of them anti-dick-chicks!" She must have struck a nerve in this nigga's ego; when, she shot him down; for him to come back with that weak-ass-shit that just pissed off the both of us but Nea more.

I balled up my fist, ready to hit this nigga, but my bitch already fucking did it first.

Her first punch alone, has this nigga damn near-folded-over; kissing his knees. My bitch is really going-in on his ass.

I look around daring any of his niggas to step in and stop her or help him because I got her back; if they do.

She punches him again; hard as fuck in his left temple and I know damn-well; he's seeing stars at this point but he manages to shake it off.

Then, suddenly this nigga makes his biggest fucking mistake; when he punches the fuck out her and all I see is blood; that's when all hell break loose.

I throw off my earrings and push him away from her and bust-that-bitch-hard-as fuck like he just did Nea a few mins ago. Blood gushes from his lip but I ain't done with this bitch yet because I punch his ass again; this time in his chin making his head snap back as I uppercut his ass.

Before I could through another punch; Nae, finally shakes back and start boxing that nigga head like a fucking punching bag; she's throwing some hard ass punches. She's drove-ass-fuck; I barely can get my punches in.

Now, it's both our fucking ass trying to tear this nigga a new asshole and still no one jumps in to stop us.

They know better than to jump in; out of nowhere, I feel a sudden sharp pain on the side of my face.

I know-this-nigga didn't; fuck playing with this nigga; now he really about to get the business; I see my chance soon as he pushes Nea back and I fucking field-goal-the fuck out the balls between his legs and start stumping-on-his-ass as soon as his knees touches the floor. Nea ass starts punching on his fucking head, while I kick him a few times in his ribs and in the back.

I hear when the door bust open, but that don't stop me; until a pair of arms is pulling me backwards; away from the bitch ass nigga.

I noticed, barely out my peripheral view; Vicious dragging Nea out of the booth, kicking and swearing.

"Man! HEN; let-me-go bruh!" I know it's pointless because I know he ain't going to let me go till I calm down.

His dad and unc help dumb ass off the floor into a nearby chair.

"Damn! y'all sho did a number on him!" His pops joke while looking at dumb ass trying to stay conscious.

I instantly calm down and feel HEN vice grip loosen from round my waist.

"So, what happened?"

His unc asks while they look around for someone to say something; but they all stay quiet.

So, I simply stated the facts. "That vanilla ass nigga got mad at Nea because she rejected his dumb ass." I respond, answering his unc question since no one else want to.

"So, because she ain't all over his dick like the rest of his thirsty hoes-he use to, he referred to her ass as a lesbian." His pops said, as he turns to everyone else in the room who nods their heads in agreement that we ain't lying.

When HEN lets me go; I already know what time it is, as he walks over to him to finish knocking his- bitch-ass out; he punches his ass in the jaw causing a loud fucking cracking sound that I know, oh too well; he just wired his jaw shut but doesn't knock him out. He hates for someone to pick on his sis for how she act. His pops roughly push him back and I grab his arm before he goes back, but his pops finishes the job of knocking him out.

"Yo! Yo! My nigga; can you hear me? You see them; nobody ever fucks with either of them." His dumbass unc yell while snapping his face as an attempt to wake him up and see his eyes open; he points back to me and over to Nea, who's now back in the booth all cozied up with Vicious arms round her.

"Because, yo-weak-ass can't handle being rejected; Now I don't want yo-bitch-ass under my management and fucking label." He yells even more pissed off than HEN; he backs away, ready for his reaction and looks as if he wanna punch on him his damn-self.

"So, yo contract is VOID with me my nigga and y'all can get this muthahfucker off my fucking property." He yells to his crew as he gets on the loudspeaker to call security.

"What's up boss?" The security guy asks as he stands in the doorway of the booth.

"Escort him and his crew the fuck out my building; they terminated of my services."

He calmly says to him as he yanks vanilla out the chair and shoves him to the security guard who drags his half conscious out booth.

"Ain't y'all leaving too?" HEN pops, yells to the vanilla crew who hesitate to leave.

Only two rush out, but this one nigga just sits there still like he deaf; the same one I say look familiar.

"What? he may be my nigga, but I can make my own paper; if you let me." He says all nonchalant like they wasn't even friends.

'That's a real nigga but a shady ass friend.' I think as I shake my head.

"Think, what y'all want but he can't put food on the table for my seeds; that's my job." He responds getting daps from both the twins, HEN and Vicious out of respect.

But forreal-forreal scratch what thought before; he a real-fucking-nigga! But; how he said that, it was like he was reading my mind; unless I said it out loud or he noticed when I was shaking my head.

"You-know-what my nigga; that built mad respect for you; on that note." Unc begin to say but I know pops bout to finish it.

"Come, to my office tomorrow at 9:30Am sharp." Pops finishes as they tag team their damn conversations like always.

"We'll talk about your contract." They surprise me when they say it at the same time doing their legendary twin power thing.

"Then, I'll bring you back here to see what you're working with." HEN unc responded back to him; with his left hand extended out to him to shake.

"Thank you, sir for this opportunity; by the way my name is Broderick James, but I go by 'Killah' in the streets." He says sounding humble as he finally tell us his name, which really has my wheels turning cause he has my last name on top the fact he looks like someone I know. I guess, I'm not the only one that notice the similarities of our last name, but no one says nothing bout it; I guess they waiting on me but it won't be today.

"I like your street name but your label name is Kilion." HEN unc responds while shaking his hand as he stands up to leave.

"Whatever you like boss, I'm just happy you're giving me a chance!" He responds as he look in my direction giving me the same look I been giving him since I noticed him in the booth, as he pass me on the way out, but quickly look away when he notices HEN looking at him sideways; I guess he didn't want him to take his actions the wrong way.

"Yo, Boss; pizzas here." I hear the security guard speaking through the loud speaker.

"OK send him to my assistant office; so she can pay and tip him. and bring the pizza down when you're done with ole dude and his pussycats crew." Pops responds back over the speakers.

"OK I'm heading your way now." The security guard replies before getting off the intercom.

Me and Nea head to the door and see him heading our direction holding 6 boxes of pizza in his hands. We quickly go to meet him half-way as we each grab our own individual box, then walks past him in the direction he just came to head to the boardroom; where we usually eat when we come and chill here.

I can hear everyone laughing at our ass but right now I don't-give-a fuck and a bitch hungry as fuck; so we just continue on walking up the hall to our destination because them lil ass BK burgers I had earlier didn't do shit.

Chapter Twenty

Ayranea's POV

Man, I just wish a nigga would stop saying that shit about me; bruh! I don't usually go HAM; I was, just-fed the fuck up. Now, we're all in the boardroom eating pizza; sort of everyone. The more I think about it, the more I get pissed off and now I'm too upset to eat that I lose my appetite.

"What's wrong shawty; I know you still ain't upset about earlier?" Vicious asked as he leans close whispering what he said in my ear.

"Why Shouldn't I be? Didn't you think the same fucking thing in class?" I snapped, getting even more upset because I yelled it in his face, since he's sitting next to me and eating out the pizza box I claimed for myself. But the look on his face and the fact he threw his pizza back in the box, he turns in his seat to face me; tells me I'm about get my ass chewed off.

"What-the-fuck! I told you in the hall earlier; if you wouldn't chop a nigga ball off every fucking time they try hollowing at you, they wouldn't fucking assume yo booshie ass gay, and if you

144

wouldn't have made that fucking comment about Mrs. Carter I wouldn't have thought the same fucking thing. Fuck! We even laughed about it; so, I thought-we-were fucking cool!"

I can't even form just one word to clap back on his ass; I was about say something until he literally tell me to "SHUT-THE-FUCK-UP-I'M NOT DONE."

"So, why-the-fuck-are-you-bringing that shit up again; because that vanilla nigga fucking rubbed-you-the-wrong-way and now, you wanna take it out on me, because I asked if you're alright?"

"Get-the-fuck-outta-here! With that petty shit; if you ain't been with a fucking female before; it's no fucking reason for you to get all fucking offended; unless you were actually with a female at some point and you fucking regretted your decision."

"Yeah, you're-fine-as fuck but your ass ain't Gawd's gift to men; if I wanted to, I can bag yo ass easily." He said all cocky and full of confidence I never seen a nigga before except in HEN; it must run in the fucking family cause I heard their pops wasn't nothing to play with when they were our age.

I'm speechless, shock, dumbfounded, and actually have a newfound respect for him; no one has ever read me like an open fucking book.

Damn! I slightly start to feel my walls crumble due to his boldness and honesty. I don't know what comes over me; when I turn his head to me and press my lips against his, making this our first kiss. At first, he just allows me to be in control; until he nips at my bottom lip; asking for access to explore my mouth with his tongue and I actually allow him to. Our lips move in sync as I deepen the kiss; suddenly, it clicks in my head, and I realized I let my walls down and kissed him.

I actually like how his tongue moves around like its playing tag with mine and it-finally-registers in my head that I actually like his preppy, cocky-ass-attitude, and outspoken boldness.

I quickly pull away and look around the room at every one's priceless and shocked expression on their faces.

They all look at me, then to him, then at each other and back to me like: 'did-she; did-he; did-they; just kiss and she kissed him first' with a dumbfounded expression on all their faces.

But when I turn to look at X'avian; he has this big ass smirk on his face, like he's saying: "yeah; I did that"; like he kissed me!

I know this nigga ain't smirking like that; I kissed-him! So, why was he acting as if; it was the other way around, like he kissed me.

Ahhh! I hate cocky fucking bastards; I raise my right eyebrow and left hand with a smirk of my own, without any warning; I simply slap the fuck out his cocky ass. He instantly replaces his smirk with an even more shocked expression than everyone else in the room.

Yea! I just slapped the smirk off his face; literally. If he thinks, it's gonna-be-that-easy-to win me over; he has another one coming. I smile innocently at him and pick up a slice of pizza, from the pizza box in front of him; with a smirk on my face, I take a big bite from it and ask: "Ain't you gonna finish eating and it's not polite to stare!"

He just stared at me in disbelief as he blinked his eyes; while he opened and closed his mouth like a fish out of water; like he wanna say something but his brain can't register anything to say.

Everyone else starts laughing their asses off at us because that was the reaction they were expecting when he put me in my place even though he was right. Because they already know that I-hate-to-be read.

"If he ain't figured it out yet, he will today; that I'm not an easy THOT; I'm a-classy-Bitch!" I say to him snapping my finger in his face.

"If he didn't know! Now, he-knows!" Everyone sings in sync; mocking a verse from one of Biggie's songs; making it an epic moment. They all burst out laughing; all except X'avian; who don't find it funny as he rubs his face.

"Aww, did witty X'avian think it was going to be easy to win me over?" I say it in a baby fide voice.

"Notttt!" I yell my point in his face at the end as I snap my finger around in the air while rolling my neck to make it all dramatic.

Call me what you want but he ain't getting it-that-easy; even if he is fine as fuck; that shit runs in the family, he has to work to win me over. Man, the twins are rolling hard in their seats laughing at their own blood; while Meekia crying and laughing at the same time.

Xav, has his 'Game-on-face' on and now, so do I.

I turn and finish eating my pizza like nothing happened; not even from what happened earlier. At least he took my mind off of that.

Part 3 –

What goes around...
comes back around...

Chapter Twenty-One

Vicious' POV

Two hours later…

After everything calmed down from the fight, Shawty kissed me first but then turned around and slapped the-fire-from-my-ass.

I realize she ain't bout to make it easy because she made it loud and clear; literally that she ain't one them easy chicks like I thought after I bumped into her in the hallway. When we finish our pizza; we all leave the boardroom heading our separate ways.

Hen, Kia and my uncle Lo'Key; head off to his office and Shawty says she has to head home till she has to pick up her sister. I offered her a ride, but she insisted she'll be fine. I gotta come up with a whole new game plan to get shawty on my team.

So, now I'm finally alone with my dad back in his office to finish talking. We're sitting, talking about my mom and he expressed how at first it was over a bet but the more time they spent together; he said he realized that he was catching feelings for her and I can tell he felt really bad about it and it was still eating up at him even to this day. I am going to show him where she buried; so, he can have some closure.

Basically, in the end, he fell deeply in love with her and tried to do what was right when he realized he caught feelings for her and she was prego with me.

He told me; he was also the reason that my mom's killer was brought to justice. He just doesn't know; that by putting him behind bars; he earned a whole new level of respect from me even if nobody else in my family ain't got respect for him. Now, I realize what I was missing in my life; my pops.

We continue talking and he tells me about his life since then; he decided he wanted to make a career in the music industry. He went to a music and performing art college. So, he could get a degree in music and entertainment. Then fresh out of college; he opened his own management and recording studio; it's called 'Gemini Entertainment, Management & Recording Studio' GEMARS for short.

"So, who are you living with?" He asks unsure how to bring up my family.

"My uncle Tate took custody of me after my mom's death." I answer nonchalantly.

"He felt like I would be too rebellious to continue to stay with my grandparents." I responded in a monotone voice.

"I read the text from my grandpa telling me to come home early; when I got there, he told me about my mom's murda and I spazzed-the-fuck out." I say as I begin to think back to that day and replay that exact moment, from my emotions, anger, and grief; I started telling him about.

"I was mad-as-fuck; I didn't wanna believe it. So, I ran out the house, got back in my car and headed straight to the hospital morgue. When, I got there I demanded that I see Kenda Moore's body; they fought me at first; the nurses tried to convince me that I didn't need to see her like that, but I didn't give-a-fuck; she was-my-mother and I just needed to see for myself; see her body with my own eyes."

At this point, I was myself in my own little Flashback as I spoke out loud to my father as I continue to play that night.

"Finally, some Dr. wearing a white lab coat on with a pin holder in his right top pocket while holding a clipboard in his left hand; come out the morgue room; asking the nurse why I'm here; but I yell out before they could answer: I just want to see my mom's body! I guess he felt I needed closure and felt I needed to identify it was her; I was grateful that he did that for me."

I started fighting back tears at this point as I tried to relive that exact moment.

"I took a deep breath and went in; all the life was drained from her body. The vibrant light brown hair was knotted up with dry blood; her blood."

I was getting choked up at this point, my mouth was getting dry; so, I don't know how I found my voice to continue speaking.

"Out of nowhere, I asked the morgue guy where she got shot and how she died. He hesitated but said she was shot in the chest; the bullet hit a main artery that caused her to bleed out internally before she realized she was shot.

In that exact moment, I felt a wave of emotions hit me like a switch turned off and that preppy-booshie persona I always portrayed; died with her. I leaned down and kissed her cold cheek, then

153

stormed out because I couldn't take it no more; I was numb.

I knew from that exact moment my life just changed; I felt like a cold blood-nigga that my unc taught me to be; was being born and I named him Vicious.

I went back home and notice no one was there; they were probably out looking for me, but I didn't give a fuck any more

This time when I walked in the house; I remember the kiss she gave me before I rushed out to school and broke down crying; I ran in her empty room and lost it.

She was really gone, you weren't around, no-one-was and I dealt with her death alone; all I had was the smell of her perfume she must have sprayed on before for work slightly lingering in the room!

I was now just a shell; I picked up her favorite pic of us that she kept on her nightstand and laid in her bed with her comforter wrapped tight around me as I cried myself to sleep.

I finished as I allow the tears to freely fall from my eyes as I feel my father wrap his arms around me, while I cry against his shoulder. I wrapped my arms round him now as I now cry hysterically like

I did that night, allowing him to comfort me like no one has since my mom's death.

He holds me till my sobs turns into silent sniffles before he pulls me over to the couch, sitting down and pulling me to sit next to him before he turns to speak:

"I'm glad you got that off your chest son; I may not have been there when you needed not just me but your family period but know I'm here from this point on."

My dad whispers in my ear.

"Holding all that in would have eaten you alive if you hadn't vented it out to someone. Trust me, I know the feeling; I held it in as well because I lost the love of my life. I felt that I would never see the child we made the night after prom. I tried finding you, I was so pissed that you were so close and yet far away because I never paid attention to the lil boy playing basketball on the other side of the court, didn't know he was my son because I never knew what she had or if she decided to keep you.

I was in the blind until your uncle brought you to the park dressed similar to my nephew; that you were my son; it was too much of a ca-wink-a-dink that y'all had the exact same outfit; just in different colors, you in red him in blue. My brother thought the same thing and when we put it together that he and Trisha, your aunt slash my brother's wife; had planned it ahead of time but it backed fired because I think I was supposed to notice you first and not him, but Trisha won't admit; we stopped asking and we couldn't ask him because he never came back to the b-court where it happen."

He finishes as he realized he lost his chance to know the truth that day.

We both seem a little more content now that we gotten our burdens off our chest, and I feel more at peace like my mom planned for us to meet; I'm also happy that I confided with my dad because I know he genuinely understands and it gave me a chance to bond with him as a father and son moment.

"Hey pops come with me for a min?" I ask him as he looks taken aback by my question but nod his head in understanding that it's time to face his demons called the Moore.

So, I made the call to my unc that I was coming home and hung up before he could respond.

Chapter Twenty Two

Laronzo's POV

I noticed my son, taking his phone from his pocket to call his people. I can tell by his facial expressions that they're not happy by the way he just; hung-up before they could respond.

"Ok! Ready-pop!" He says a lil too perky for my likings; this nigga was just about to smash his phone, just a few-mins-ago, looking all angry and shit; before he hung up. Now, he's all happy; like nothing just happened but I can see fire behind his eyes as he tries to keep his cool about it...'tries'' the hint keyword.

Have you ever heard of the saying; "it's always calm before a storm comes." Well. I sure hope they prepared for hurricane Laronzo and tornado X'avian heading straight for their ass.

It was only supposed to be a thirty minutes ride, if he wouldn't have taken the bus route; had he known that; he would've turned left on Canal Ave; where my studio is, continued to 8th, turned right at the light of 8th and Brisher Blvd then turned left instead of a right on his street Wislen Ave.

It would have cut 15min off, instead he went back towards his school, BK and to his house that way; his school is ten min from me, BK is fifteen, and the school is another 15min from his house. It took us 40 minutes the way with the route just took but he was only back tracking the route he knows. Saying I'm nervous and pissed; all at the same fucking time is an understatement; we could have walked there. Man, I feel like shooting first and talking later; but I didn't bring my peace maker and it wouldn't have solved anything.

"Pops! you alright over there?" He asks me as I'm subconsciously clenching and unclenching my fist. This nigga uncle lived so fucking close to my shit; it ain't-even funny.

"Yeah, I'm good but pissed as fuck right now." I honestly responded to him because he's had enough people lying to him in his life; he doesn't need another one from me as well.

He parks in the driveway but before he can cut the engine off to his car; another one pulls up on side him; since it's a two-car driveway.

"Better now then never; right!" I crack a joke to calm us both down; we both burst out laughing as we get out of the car at the same time.

SMACK!!! I suddenly hear ringing in my ears as I realized someone just tried to slap fire out my ass.

"Grandma! what you do that for; he ain't did shit!" I hear as I shake back to my sense; I notice Mrs. Moore just a few feet from me being held back from by her husband, my son yelling in her face, and oddly his uncle Tate with this relieved look on his face almost like nigga wanted to laugh and put this shit on the FB live action.

I wouldn't put it past him because he subconsciously planned this shit to come out. By the look on his face; he looks as though he could die a happy man right now.

"Yo! Earth to Laronzo!" X'avian yell in my face; startling the fuck out of me. I was so dazed out; I didn't even notice him standing in front me or that everyone else had already headed in the house.

"Nigga! damn I ain't deaf; I can hear-yo-ass fuck!" I say to hide the fact that I actually didn't because I was so dazed out.

"Whatever; I've been trying to get your attention now for like 10min-pops; but you ain't 'deaf" though. She must've slapped ya hearing aid out den." He says as he fake like he looking for something on the ground.

"Sarcastic-Bastard!" I say under my breath, but he must have heard me because he replies back with a slick remark.

"Hey, takes one to know one!" I roll my eyes at his ass because he reminds me of myself.

"Nigga! Bring yo-ass on; so, we can get this shit over with." I respond as I shove pass him, when I hear this nigga laughing alongside me as we walk towards the lion's den.

Chapter Twenty Three

Tate's POV

Bruh! I feel like I can finally die a happy man; not literally of course but you see my logic right. Everything seemed to be happening faster than I planned; I forgot but counted on him bumping into his cuzin at the school. I just figured, he'll come to me first; then eventually, he'll want to meet his pops since his studio is 30min away but instead he went a whole different route than I expected. Well, no better time to do then the present; shit I'm tired of putting on a persona I'm not.

My mom is sitting all pissed and puffed up because she is still pissed off at Ghost for breaking my sister's heart, getting her pregnant and not being there for his son. What she doesn't know is that; it's all my father's fault.

At times, he came at me trying to get to her since the day at the park; that's why I had to switch parks and the fact that my dad heard what happened. He threatened to build a dirty case on him that had enough bullshit pinned up on him that he should be doing ten life sentences. The only reason he's not; is because I had convinced him she didn't live in Chicago and to leave the sleeping dog lying because eventually he'll meet him again. I quickly glance at the man that raised me up in his lies and I can tell from the look in his eyes that he is thinking of how to finally get rid of me.

Suddenly his demeanor changes, when he looks up to see Ghost and Xav laughing together as they walk through the door; I guess he never pictured them ever being in the same room.

Ghost closes the door as he looks around the room at my parents' pissed off faces and X'avian's confused expression. I can tell he is trying to hide his anger and I don't blame him.

From the beginning, I wanted no part in lying to him and I'm not going to from this point on anymore; "my obligations to lie to him ended on his 18th birthday which passed a month before his mom died". I say those exact words out loud soon as they all look at me like: What-the-fuck I'm talking about expressions on their faces; all except, my dad who already knows; what I'm about to confess.

I stand up from my seat; looking directly at him when I say: "All your skeletons are about to come out the closest and I did my part when I kept my promise that I made to God as soon as I saw you in my rear-view mirror." I say pointing my finger at Laronzo at the end.

"After, I left the park when I almost lost my life over your lies!" I yell while pointing at my damn parents; my dad in particular. My dad tries to hide the fact that he's guilty as fuck by looking all pathetic because he knows I am fucking right.

"I left that day with my scared and crying nephew still on the floor of my car; I knew at that point, I had to fix y'all wrong."

"When, I got him home and told his mom what happened; she was pissed and called my father".

"Who told me, I could never fucking see or take you out again and my father then said: if I ever told your father where you were; he would deal with my trouble making behavior."

"So, I moved an hour away from Chicago under the watchful eyes of Commissioner Moore and the only reason I came back; was because I heard the announcement of my for-sister's death being broadcasted on the news."

I noticed my nephew's facial expression is a mix of confusion and anger, I then turn to my parents hoping my father gets what I'm saying.

"I promised God that when he turns 18 all the lies, I kept for my family, I was gonna let them skeletons out the closet."

I say out loud at the end as I turn back to my nephew.

"X'avian, I always loved you like my own but it wasn't my place to tell you something that your mom could have told you when you were old enough to understand. I made damn sure you never turn out like them."

I continue as I point my finger at my father.

"My place in your life was like a father figure; he gave that role to me. It wasn't a role I would have chosen for myself. I wanted to tell you from day one; ever since you called me 'dada' about your pops. But, no one wanted to hear the truth from the black-sheep of da family. Yes, I referred to myself as the black-sheep; because I'm nothing-like-them."

I mumble out loud to myself but enough for everyone to hear.

"But after having a gun pointed at my head over lies, I was forced to keep, was enough for me; that's why, I stopped coming around because I had no choice."

"I know this is going to sound cold hearted; but hell, I'm glad she's gone because she's not here to stop me from letting you know the truth. She was so brainwashed by our father's lies; that she kept your father out of your life because he fed her lies.

Lies that your father just wanted her for sex and that he only acted like he loved her. When she found out she was pregnant; he fed her lies that he would never step-up to take care of his child and that he didn't deserve to have him in his life.

He tried everything in his power to get her to have an abortion, but she was too stubborn. Then, she actually went to do it, but she found out she was in her second trimester and was having a boy, while lying on the abortion table; she couldn't kill you because of the love she still had for your father. My father had no choice but to accept it, but she couldn't stay in his house anymore; he put her out and she lived with me till she had you and was able to get her own place."

Chapter Twenty Four

"Suddenly, out of the blue he came back in her life; I knew it was only because he wanted to make sure, she wouldn't try to bring your dad around you to raise, because wanted me and him to be the father figures in your life. They would have never told you no matter how rebellious you got."

I feel like a weight has been lifted off my shoulders; my dad I'm surprised never stepped in to say anything to stop my confession, but I guess if he does, it would be proving…. I'm right but I guess I haven't pressed the right buttons; yet.

"He ruined my life of being an uncle to my own nephew, my career and having a life of my own."

I say to no one in particular as I feel myself getting a little choked up at this point; Ghost looks at me with pity because of the shit he realized I went through.

This where I know, I am going to get a reaction from him; this is the secret that he built all his lies around to become the Commissioner.

"I'm not even their blood son; naw I'm ya nephew; ain't that-right-Unc!"

166

I confess to my nephew who looks shocked as fuck as his pops.

"I'm your brother's son; who went to jail for the lies you told to put him there! How does an ex-dope dealer turn into a dirty cop and get promoted to an even dirtier commissioner?"

I ask in a questionable tone as I answer my own question by saying:

"Easy, he let his own brother take the fall for him, pin all his criminal history on him and let him rot in jail till his sudden death."

I smirk seeing the look on my uncle's face; cat's out the bag now bruh, and I don't even give a fuck right now.

"You thought I didn't know huh; tiss-tiss Unc; the streets talk, and just because you have shit to hold over them that could put them in jail for life. It doesn't mean shit; until you have a gun pointed to your head. I also know you're the reason my mom killed herself; she found out how scandalous the Moore's men are; at least that's what a little birdy told me."

"Lavon Tate that's enough; your father was never any drug dealer; he went out and worked hard to provide for his…...."

I hurry and cut her off quick as I say:

"See mom or should say auntie; that's where you're wrong. He kept you in the house and away from the mouths in the street and you being the naive wife of all times; never paid attention to anything he did. Shit, for all I know you could have known and just didn't give a fuck long as the money was coming in.

Who doesn't cry at their own sister's funeral; you could have been involved in her suicide-murder. Who marries someone they know nothing about? No loose ends right; Cassius Milton Moore!"

I say as the kettle finally starts singing; now I've gotten the reaction I've been waiting for all night, not just from him but Ghost as well. I ain't got long now before he snaps and ends my life; like he does everyone who expose his real name, but this show ain't over yet, but this will blow the house down.

"Cassius Moore aka C-Bone Milton; the biggest dope dealer in Chicago and the same muthafucker; who had my pops killed!"

Ghost suddenly yells out as he tries to launch at my father; but Xav holds him back as I continue throwing gasoline on the fire.

"Yep! that's him, the same dirty cop who pinned every crime he committed and people he murdered on his own brother and kills anybody who can't keep their mouth shut."

I yell at the man who fucking raised me from one years old, taught me about the street and took my pops and mom from me. I finally got everything off my chest; I feel beyond relief of my confession to my nephew, Ghost and my naive aunt.

"You son-of-bitch; I knew I should've gotten rid of your dumb-ass like that naive fucking daughter of mine and whore of a mother of yours!"

He yells back at me as he confesses he had something to do with their death; just like I knew he-fucking-would.

"She wanted out; so, I gave her the only way out. She wouldn't listen; she slept with the son of my street rival and had that bastard child for him!"

He screams out loud because he's pissed for being called out and forgetting my nephew sitting in the room with his enemy's son or it may just be; he don't give a fuck at this point.

"Your pops was my only biggest competition in the street; and he was trying to come up on my side of town trying to get greedy; so yeah, I took his ass out the game."

He just says, not giving a fuck that he just confessed to Ghost in his face that he killed his pops; again, I stepped between them because I'm for sure if he had a gun he would have been dead.

It took me a min to calm him down and to stop him from going after him; I bet he wishes now he was strapped.

"Karma-fucking-stabbed me in the back, when I saw y'all together; I knew as soon as I saw your face who son you were. Then you had to talk the lil slut out her panties, I was even more mad, when she told me she was keeping my enemy's son seed; your bustard baby."

He says with no remorse and is filled with nothing but venom and hatred in his voice as he refers to my nephew being a bastard's child and mistake.

Everyone in the room, finally see what I've known since I was old enough to learn about the game, which he taught me. That this nigga has no fucking heart to say what he just said, and confessed in this room to everyone here.

My mom begins to cry because she realized all these years what she was married to. As I turn to check and say something to X'avian; I notice him reach behind his back as he pulls out his Glock nine.

"I paid my way to get to the top and nobody is about to change that; I'll kill-every-fucking-one of y'all! Starting with yo snitching ass."

He yells as he points the gun in my direction as he cocks it back; I quickly pull out mine and point it back at him.

POW!!! I hear the sound of a single shot of a gun going off, but it doesn't feel like I was shot. Suddenly, I see my uncle's lifeless body falling to the floor with a single shot to the chest, but it looks more like an exit wound.

I first look at Xav but he's looking as shocked as me while staring in my aunt's direction. I follow his gaze and gasp at her holding a .22LR mini-mag handgun; that she used to finally shoot the fucking bastard she knew as her husband. She began crying hysterically because she just realized; she was married to a fucking monster.

POW! POW!! POW!!! POW!!!! POW!!!!! POW!!!!!!; CLICK! CLICK!!CLICK!!!

She fires again and again until she empties the whole barrow of her gun into her husband's corpse while she continue to cry over his sorry fucking body. I'm too in shock to do anything; suddenly, I start firing my own damn gun at his corpse out of fucking anger, but I don't use all my bullets.

X'avian runs over to console my aunt while Ghost looks as though he's still trying to process everything.

I drop to my knees because I finally feel free but now my life is ruined, and I don't have shit to live for anymore because I'll be behind bars.

"Bruh, take care of my nephew please." I say to Ghost as he tries to come over as an attempt to take my gun, but I quickly point it at him while shaking my head. He just nodded in understanding as I put the gun up to my temple.

Mentally, I say goodbye to my nephew crying in his father's arms because he had to stop him from stopping me; I glance at the woman who raised me and mumble "I love you!"

I shake my head no, as she tries to run and stop me but that just motivates me to pull the trigger faster, to use the last bullet on myself. I quickly press down till I hear a click and the bullet vibrating down the barrow.

CLOWL!!! The sound of my Glock 9×19mm is the only sound I could hear, before I close my eyes to accept my fate.

I feel the bullet passing through my skull as my life flashes before my eyes. It begins, when I realized I was an uncle to Xav, meeting Prat; who I always looked at as a big brother to me, and lastly my first love I had to sacrifice, after my unc ruined my basketball career; Chrystal Wismen. I heard the rumors of her being a gold-digger and her pregnancy and I held on to that moment; because it gave me hope of a possibility that I may be leaving a part of me behind, as everything suddenly goes black. I take my last breath before my body can hit the floor and I welcome my eternity in hell.

Chapter Twenty Five

Unknown POV

I couldn't listen to anything else; how could I be so naive to miss the signs. 38yrs I was married to a monster; I had my suspensions, gut-feeling, and ignored the coldness in his voice. I lived a lie and I loved his dirty-draws and money he was being in. My poor baby girl; she loved that young man and he kept her away from him only because of the mess he caused in the streets with this young man's father and now I feel bad for slapping him.

I see my husband's hand moving slowly behind his back as he pulls out his gun; he quickly-jumps-up from the couch and points it in my son's direction. Oh-my-God! he-about to shoot my baby; I know he ain't mine by blood but I raised him. I quickly dug in my purse for my .22LR mini-mag handgun that he gave me for protection; without anyone noticing me and I fired once without no hesitation and shot him in the back of his chest when I heard him cock his gun.

I watch him turn his head around shocked that I would shoot him as his lifeless body falling to the floor

I stare at him as everything seems to move in slow motion as I watch him fall to his knees first then forward as he falls on his stomach without the gun going off as it hits the floor next to him.

I stare at his back slowly rise; he's still alive and I get angry at him for all the lies.

Before I realize it I empty the barrow of my gun in his; now lifeless corpse.

I feel this weight lifted off me and I finally feel free.

No more pretending to be a happy wife, hiding the abuse behind closed doors; all the bruises I tried to hide and seeing my family suffer at his hands of this monster.

Suddenly I hear more shots fired and know it's from my son's gun.

My grandson comes over and takes the gun from my shaking hands as he drops it beside, me then helps me to sit on the couch holding me as I cry. Cassius may have put me through hell, even took everything from me, and though I lived in his lie he created for his family for almost 40yrs; I still can't help but love him.

Suddenly I hear more shots being fired; he kept this a secret for so long. I know it was a big burden for him to bear; that's his way of letting it go finally.

I let my grandson know I'm ok as I get up to console him, but before I can get over to him; I see Tate whisper something to X'avian's father as he points the gun to his head. I also see X'avian rush pass me to stop him as well but his father snatches him up before he can reach him as he cries in his father's arm because he stopped him from trying to take the gun. It's in that moment that I realized that he has nothing to live for, and I scream:

"NO LORD! PLEASE NOT HIM TOO!" I tried to run to him, but I see in his eyes that no matter what actions I take or what I attempt to say, he still has nothing to live for and that my actions was the motivation he needed to pull the trigger and I wouldn't have reached him in time anyway; but I try anyway, only to hear his gun go off, making a:

POW!!!

I stop in my track and watch the bullet passes through his skull and see his brain splattering on the wall behind him as his gun falling from his hands. I drop to my knees as everything begins to move in slow motion before his body slams to the floor knocking his last breath from his lifeless body.

I begin crying hysterically because I'm hurt, broken, and numb as I slowly begin to crawl over to but stop when I hear the sirens in the background; I know they are far enough for to apologize to this young man and I hope he can find it in his heart to forgive for the pain my husband caused his family; I turn to him getting his attention when I call him by the name I heard my nephew call him

"Ghost! Y'all need to go; please take care of him please. I'm sorry for everything; I didn't know he was living a double life and I'm so sorry now, please go before they get here."

 I tell him as he looks at me with understanding and forgiveness as he mouths; "I forgive you." making feel relieved and grateful as I continue on by saying: …

"I'll explain everything; he has a security camera that will explain everything."

"I'll be ok; PLEASE! Go! GO! NOW!"

Finally, he nods head in understanding and drags my crying grandson out the door with him.

I sigh a breath of relief as I hear his car pull out the driveway.

I can hear the siren getting closer as I slowly crawl over to my nephew; I gently pick up his mutilated head and place it in my lap.

While some people would be sick from the sight of his half blown off head; all I see is my son I never had. While I cry again over his body; I hear the footsteps of the cops rushing through the doors.

"Carlene what happened here, who did this?"

The officer that I know all too well; askes me as he calls me by name because he knows me as a well known judge, the police Commissioner's wife and because we been messing around for the past 10yrs. I'm not surprised he was the first to come in, but I can't find my voice to speak; so instead I just point to the security cam in the corner of the room.

"Go get the tapes!" He yells at one of the other officer in the room.   "Go get the tapes!"

He yelled at one of the other officers in the room.

"Come on Carlene; we need...."I cut him off by saying...

"Come on Carlene; we need...."

I cut him off by saying: "I know the procedure; Officer Hallan!"

I say to him, putting my feelings aside for him as I speak to him in a professional manner to show respects to my dead husband in the room. He just nodded in understanding while he waited for me to get up on my own; I place a kiss on my son's cheek and notice he has his hand extended out to help me stand; which I accept appreciatively.

He just nodded and while he waited for me to get up on my own.

I place a kiss on my son's cheek and notice the officer extends his hand to help me up.

"You don't have to read my rights; I know them by heart."

"I can't do that Mrs. Carlene; the rules apply to everyone in this kind of situation." He responds with a hint of pain in his voice as he read me my Miranda's right. I nod my head in understanding because I know there's certain protocols that he has to follow; I just never thought it'll be to me.

He proceeded to read me my rights.

"Carlene you have the right to remain silent anything you say can and will be used against you in a court of law. You have the right to an attorney;

if you cannot afford an attorney, one will be appointed."

I tone out the rest as I look down at my son.

"Can you cuff my hands in front me please?" I ask him politely when he's done; nod his head as he reaches behind his back and grab his cuffs and proceed to put them on my wrist.

"Please be careful with him please." I say to the morgue assistant as he bends down to examine my son.

The officer leads me outside to his patrol car; as the CSI crew pass by us heading inside to do their part. He opens the door for me to get in; I'm thankful that he helps me in and closes it once I pull my legs in. I say a sight prayer for my son and grandson, as the officer gets in behind the wheel and drives off toward the station.

Chapter Twenty-Six

Laronzo's POV

I didn't know the events of this evening would have ended like that; I didn't bother going back to the studio so instead I took him home.

"Hi baby, did you hear what happened on the news?"

I hear my wife Liza ask from the kitchen soon as she heard me walk in, as she walks into the hallway leading to the foyer, and notices X'avian crying hysterically in my arms. She looks at how broken he is and connects the pieces; she doesn't say a word as she walks over to us and wraps him in her arms.

He turns from me to her when he feels her embrace and cry even harder. I chuckled to myself as I noticed that he towers over her short frame.

"I know baby it hurts right now, but I'm here for you; I can't replace your mom and won't try to, but I'll be the mother figure you need." I hear her whisper in his ears as they stand a few feet from me; he seems to calm down and nods his head.

"Daddy your home; who's this?"

My 10yr old daughter asks as Xavian looks over Liz's shoulders to see her.

Liz steps away about to introduce the two of them until she noticed the look in his face as he looks at me confused, then pissed and suddenly sad all in one blink; he has got to be bipolar because his mood changes too fucking quick for my likings.

He looks at me briefly then to Liza and over to Mariah before he begins to back away from all of us; I already know what he's thinking that I lied to him because I didn't mention them earlier doing our talk.

"X'avian, wait it's not what you think."

But he storms out grabbing his keys from my hand and runs out the door and I realize he has a problem with running from his problems.

I know he's either going to find HEN or he's going to go to the cemetery to vent to his mom...so I pick the cemetery and text HEN to meet me there just in case he doesn't want to talk to me.

"Go after him dumbass! Don't just stand there looking stupid!"

Liz screams in my face as she slaps me in the back of my head, punches me a few times in the chest while I was trying to finish sending Darian the damn text.

"Damn woman! I'm going! Damn-Mother-Fucking-Hen!"

She gave me this, "don't fucking try me" look that I know all too well, and I quickly grab her car keys from the table since my car still at the studio.

X'avian's POV

I didn't leave because he had a whole family he didn't mention to me when he had the chance earlier; I left because my mom kept me from him and my sister.

What if she was my age and we met, started messing around and then we found out when I went to ask for her hand in marriage that we have the same dad... just thinking about it made me sick to the stomach.

I don't know how I made it here cause I don't know much about this side of town; so I rode around till something looked familiar and found the route I know like the back of my hand.

I park the car and sit there for a few min before I get out and walk to her grave and sit down in front of her grave.

"Hey Mom; I know you saw everything that happened, and you should feel like shit... you should have listened to Uncle, well our cousin Tate and not Cassius.... who does that to his own blood Bruh forreal...I can't believe I looked up to him; but anyway I wish I wouldn't have never ignored that feeling I was having before I left for school. I should have had breakfast with you, talked with you longer, should have..."

I try to continue but I'm too choked up and begin to cry…

"Mom, I have no one; grandma I'm sure going to jail, uncle left me in the hands of a man I just found out is my father, but he already has a family! Did y'all think of me; how it would affect me when y'all dirty laundry got ironed out…Y'all were selfish as fuck! I don't fucking have no one mom!" I yelled angry ass fuck as I punch the grown.

"Yo, cuz you have me."

I damn near jump out my skin when I hear his voice; I quickly turn around and wonder how much he heard as I see him walking up to me with pity in his eyes. He doesn't say much else as he sits next to me in front of my mom's tombstone with her pic engraved on it.

"Your mom was really a beautiful woman; I see why unc fought so hard to be with her."

He says as I notice the admiration in his eyes as he silently read her bio on her headstone.

"So ummm how you found me?" I ask him curiously.

"Your dad figured if you couldn't find me; you'll come here, so we've been riding to each one till we found you. I text him a few min ago you were at 'Precious Garden of Memories' I wasn't at first going to interrupt but I couldn't let you feel like you're alone."

He said as he sat facing me.

"You may not remember but we used to be close! Your uncle started bringing you to the park with him soon as you could walk; we would play like we were tall enough to shoot the ball in the hoop. If someone picked on you, they got dealt with by my crew that were a few years older than us...you just turned 18, right?"

He asked as I stared at him dumbfounded cause he knew how old I was.

"Yeah, now you know. Mine is two months later on the same day; but I'll be 20..." He responds like he knew what I was thinking.

"Wow so when I was two you were four; born on the same day two months and two years apart." I respond doing the math of how close we could be to twins born two years after apart.

"We're almost twins!"

We say at the same time, as we sit in a comfortable silence until we heard a buzzing sound of his phone being on vibrate.

"Hey, your pops just buzzed my pocket and said he's waiting in the car to talk to you."

I nod my head downwards to tell him it's ok, then I notice HEN takes his phone to send him a text that it's ok to come.

He stands up next to me when he notices my dad walking up the path to us.

"I'll be back in the car; Nea told me to call her when I found you; she has been worried since we all saw the news."

"Thanks Bro!"

He nods in response knowing we're not actual Bros, but I see him like one.

"No prob!" He responded as he left to give us some privacy when he noticed my father standing behind him.

He approaches me cautiously without saying a word; I don't know if it's because it's my mother's grave or he thinks I may blow up on him.

"Dad, it's ok she won't come out the grave to fuck you up, if she do, you're on ya muthafucking own my nigga, cause I'm leaving yo ass with my dust!"

I say jokingly as he stop as if it would really happen; I tried not to but I fucking burst out fucking laughing so hard that I started crying, my stomach started cramping up, and my jaw damn near locked up. As I smile when I notice him relax a little before joining me on the ground in front my mom's grave.

"That's a nice pic of your mom; she still looks the same."

He says as he notices the pic I chose for her headstone that she took on my birthday.

"I know we just met and you think you have no one, but you have, me, Liza and Mariah; yeah she's your half sis. Me and Liza almost got divorced the day your mom died."

I was going to ask why, then notice my mom's middle name 'Mariah.'

"You named her after my mom; wow you really did love her." I say as I look at him with admiration.

"Sort of, I named her Mariah Kendranette."
He responds with pride in his voice.

"Why though?" I asked curiously, really wanting to know his answer as I wait for his response.

"It was the same reason she named you after me; to keep a drunken promise that showed how much we loved each other, as a way to have a part of them around."

I look at him like he done lost his damn mind as I say:

"I-would-have-divorced yo-ass too! That's-like a slap in-the-face to her; you-named-your daughter-with-your-new love of-your-life after the-first love-of-your-life as a reminder of her-to keep a-drunken-promise…"

I say while I drag out each word as I try to explain in it layman's term:

"I'm surprised yo ass ain't laying next to my mom on that note; bruh!"

I finished making it clear if it was me he would be in the afterlife with my mom.

"Damn, I didn't think of it that way." He responds as my words start to sink in.

"Were you drunk when they asked you to name her?" I asked as I look at him, he grew a third head.

"Boy no, but I promised if we had a girl or boy together, that's how we would name them." He said, still not getting the point.

"I can understand why mom kept her side of the promise, but y'all wasn't even-together-when you named-your-daughter-you had-with-another-woman after a-woman you-loved-in high-school, had-a one-nightstand with from-a-jock-bet and you-wasn't-even-drunk-when-you named her but your excuse was: and I quote 'to keep a drunken promise, to show her how much we loved each other, as a way to have a part of them around' unquote."

I said again, while dragging the word in layman's term. While I'm trying to make a valid point.

"Dad you're still in love with my mom and married Liza because she has qualities of my mom, because Liza can pass for the older version of my mom as her doppelganger; Especially when you noticed my picture and when I remembered Liza's face."

I say to him as he sits there speechless, as my words begin to sink in.

He looks like he's seen a ghost when I pointed out the close resemblance of my mom and Liza and why he kept the promise with my mom. I hear him mumbling shit incoherently until I hear him say:

"She can never see your mom's grave, I literally I won't be leaving with you because she's going to bury me on top her." He says under his breath, as I strongly agreed with him, although I know eventually she will fund out.

"So, What Liz is going to do about the origin of Mari's name?" I ask still curious.

"We decided to leave it as it is for now and let Dranette decide if she wants to change it when she is old enough to understand the story of her name."

He says feeling embarrassed that he realized he never stopped loving mom and by doing so married a woman who looks like an older version of her.

"Mom, what you do to this nigga; put that good-good on that he went and name his daughter after you and married an older look alike version of you, because he couldn't marry the original copy."

I say jokingly as he hit me a little too hard in my arm to call it playfully, because he knows everything I said is the pure truth, and she left a brand on his heart to do some dumb shit like that.

"So, what now...?"

I say, as I stand up to stretch my legs.

"You're coming to live with us till you finish high school and then we're shipping yo ass off to college!"

He responds as he stands up as well.

"Shit sounds like a plan; Liza I bet wanted to strangle your ass when I left huh..."

I say playfully as we stand in the same spot.

"Naw! She was too worried about you, that she was beating my ass out the house to find you; not that I wasn't but she didn't give me time to get help. I only had time to connect with HEN because he was all over my phone trying to tell me about you, and she said not to come home without you. So! Let's go before she comes looking for the both of us and bury my body when she finds me here with you, and notice your mom's headstone." He says in a serious but jokingly tone.

"Wow! Yeah, she went into mother hen mode as soon as she saw you."

He says making me feel proud that I lost a booshie fam to only have them replaced with one who accepts me and will love me like my mom, unc, and grandma did.

"Mom, I love you and Thank you; dad, let's go home because I'm hungry as fuck!"

I say to her headstone as we both lean down and kisses the top of her headstone, then I follow behind him as he gets in his car, while I get into mine and follow him on his route back home which only took 30 min maybe 40.

"Did you find him because if not you can walk yo ass right back out that got damn door until you do; now where is he?"

I hear Liza saying exactly what dad said she would, as she bombard him with questions about me as soon as he walked in.

I tried so hard to not laugh, but I couldn't hold it in and burst out laughing as I follow her rambling to the living room as she paces back and forth until she notices me.

"Baby are you ok? if you need to talk I'm here don't...."

I cut her off rambling and pulled her into my arms; she's taken by surprise at first, but then wraps her around me hugging me back. She reminds me so much of my mom's caring nature, making it easier for me to warm up to her.

I pull away and notice Mariah the only one not in the room; Liz notices and lets me know she went to bed an hour ago.

"You're hungry, there's some leftovers in the fridge?" She asked when she hears my stomach growling.

"Naw if you have some cereal that'll be fine." She burst out laughing as I looked dumbfounded at her; curious behind why she's laughing until I hear what she says under her breath.

"Yeah! Ronzo that's your child; all y'all ass live off junk food!" I hear my dad laughing at her comment as it dawns on me that she was referring y'all to me, dad and Mari.

"Come on son, I'll show you to your room then tomorrow I'll get you a laptop, notebook, any game system you want, a new phone, switch your insurance over to mine, and take you shopping for some new clothes and shoes."

He says in one breath as we head up a set of stairs to the second floor, as he takes a right while I follow behind him as he lead me to my new room.

"What about the stuff at my Unc's house? I have my fav pic of me and my mom in my room and a few pics of my unc that I also want to get…"

I say, starting to get nervous that I can't get my things from my house.

"What about the money that my uncle funded for grants and scholarships that I'm sure he left for me if anything happened to him."

I rant on about the money he had and left for me; none of which I cared about like that; he helped a lot of kids get in college through his scholarship programs and I want to keep that, to make sure I continue his legacy.

"Hey, we'll talk with a lawyer tomorrow about all your unc finances, wills, business, houses, cats, and belongings tomorrow. I'll also talk to the homicide office in charge of your grandma's case and ask if the forensic team would let you use your key to get everything that you want once they're done cleaning the house. Then we can sort out the rest once you're in a better mindset."

He tells me, setting my mind at ease for now.

"We'll handle that in the morning." He says to me, as we finally make it to the guestroom that will soon be my room.

"Ok." I respond as I begin to settle in my new room that he showed me as mine.

It has a King size bed, 55" wall mounted curve HD flat screen with wall to wall surround sound speakers in every corner of the room, huge walk-in closet empty for now, a desk, and adjoined personal bathroom with an 32" flat screen.

A walk-in shower with spa massage spout, jet stream Jacuzzi tub and button flush toilet; yo the bathroom is dope as fuck with a normal stainless steel bowl and motion sensor faucets sink with a head mirror.

'Bruh this is better than my old room. I'm excited that I don't have to share a bathroom anymore.' I think to myself after my dad show me around the bedroom and bathroom that I know for sure will be my favorite room.

"So you like your room?" Liz asks as she hands me a bowl of my favorite cereal; Cinno Toast Crunch.

"Let me guess, this is his favorite cereal?"

"Nope! Actually, it's mine and usually I don't share but your father hid his and Mari ate the last box of hers; so, I had no choice."

She says popping the "P" when she said nope making me laugh though because dad actually hides his cereal and Mari ate her last box like she had a choice of more than one. I get from the chair to give her a hug as I sit back down at my desk to devour what's left before they get soggy.

"Thank you for sharing your box with me but umm would you mine if I put a mini fridge in here?" I ask her out the blue as she look at me dumbfounded till I explained that I wanted it for my milk, juice and soda I definitely don't want any one touching.

"Oh ok! I feel you on that, so I guess till I get some more Cinno Toast Crunch we'll be sharing." She responds, sounding disappointed at the end that she has to share her box of cereal.

"Hey! I go through 10 box a month of the family value; shit, I hope you have enough." I tell her as she looks like she wanna withdraw her offer but nod and say:

"Yep, definitely going shopping at Sam's, BJ, and Costco for groceries from now on!"

She responds making me and pops laugh.

"Get some rest; the principle said take as much time as you need; your teachers will email me all your class work and HEN will bring and turn in any assignments that you have to do for the two classes y'all have together."

She says as I look at confused as to how she already knows what school I attend; she must have read my facial when she responds:

"He's, my dad!" In a perky nonchalant tone. Wow, now I see the resemblance, who would have thought.

"Well I'll leave you be, me and your father have some things to talk about…Not all about you but you're somewhere in there!" She says as she takes the empty bowl after I finished the last of my cereal to the kitchen.

 My father lingers around the room waiting for me to say something to him, until he hears Liz coming back up the stairs and his face has the grim look as to say: 'time to face the music.'

"Goodnight, pops!" I say, giving with a hint of: 'get the fuck out!' tone in my voice as he leaves, once he gets the hint that he needed to leave. He doesn't say anything as he closes the door behind; I quickly take off everything except my boxers,

then go to turn the light off and climb in bed;
falling asleep soon as my head hit the pillow.

Chapter Twenty Seven

Hen's POV

"Breaking news tonight; the honorable Judge Carlene Moore is being charged for the murder in self-defense and enraged overkill of her husband and Chicago's Police Commissioner, Cassius Moore aka C-Bone Milton. Father to the late Kenda Moore; who was killed a few months ago in an armed robbery; but we now know it was a staged murder by the late Commissioner to keep his secret from getting out."

The news report announces, as we watched the 5pm news broadcast.

"Turns out the late Commissioner was also Chicago's bigger drug lord but ran the streets using his father's last name, which was Milton. The Commissioner a few years back pinned all drug trafficking, murders, and claimed the reason for the crime on the streets; was all because of his late brother, Deondrick Moore. Who was the father of his late nephew, who he raised since the murder suicide of Alison Winton-Moore; his brother's late wife and mother of his nephew."

We listened in shock as the news anchor ladies continued...

"Lavon Tate Moore was a former Celtics player; whose career ended all too soon because of a ploy by his uncle as a form of punishment for his rebellious behavior as the Police Commissioner's son; but that did not stop Mr. Moore from giving back to the community, because he was the owner of: 'Moore To Give Community Center and Gyms' all around Chicago's urban areas; In an effort to give hope to the less fortunate youth of his childhood Community. He was also one of the victims found tonight in the gruesome murder scene; placed in his own home."

The report takes a sec to regain her composure as she continues.

"All cases handled by the late Commissioner will be reopened and reviewed by the FBI; any officers, judges, lawyers, ect....that were involved in any wrongly conviction by the Commissioner as a cover will be brought to justice or finally released. There is no word of the Commissioner's grandson X'avian McTyson who was fled the scene with an unknown man, moments before the policed arrived. The neighbor who called 911 told the police that he witnessed them fleeing from in his car. X'avian McTyson is the son of the late

Kenda Moore that we mentioned earlier in our story. As of now no charges are being filed on him; since he was an innocent bystander witnessed everything with the unknown man because everything was caught on a security tape that made this an open shut case. Thank you for listening, we will keep you updated with more on this story in tomorrow's news. I am Finesha Yang; good night, Chicago."

The anchor lady finishes, leaving us looking flabbergasted as we stare blankly.

"Damn! My nigga life just changed forever in one fucking day" My pops say as he grabbed the remote and turned it off while everyone else just stares at the TV screen including myself, until I get a text from my Unc saying Xav ran off somewhere and he thinks he may have gone to the cemetery where his mom is buried. I only know of two between the school and where I am now, because it's close to Booshieville where he used to live. I text him back letting him know I'll check those first while he checked other one on the other side of town.

"Darian, where are you going?" Nea asks, concerned when she notices I grab my keys and tries to rush to the door before she tries to stop me.

"I gotta go help my Unc look for Xav." I say as I tried stepping around her because she standing in front the door.

"I'm coming too!" She says as she tries to follow behind me.

"Naw! Man he needs someone he can trust; not saying he doesn't trust you but this is more of a family matter; now move I have to go!"

I say as I slightly shove her out the way.

"Call me when you find him!" She says almost in tears; damn, I've never seen her this emotional over a nigga and her actions just confirmed there was a connection between those two and right now she's going to have to hold him down and pull him out his fuck because he needs a ROD chick.

"I got you sis, or should I say fam!"

I say to her as I leave her open to correct to see when she catches on to what I'm insinuating about her now being his girl and actually in the fam; she just nods her head as she yells:

"Now go find my man!" In a serious tone that has me turning around quick as fuck because that's her 'I'll fuck a bitch up over mine!' Damn! Boy he just pull the hardest baddie in school; man; them two mutha-fuckers was made for each other.

I went to the one closest to me, since I already lost a lot of time talking with Nea and was happy that I decided to follow my first mind, because I found him at Precious Garden of Memories, and ever since we been tighter than a pair of draws on an elephant's ass.

Chapter Twenty Eight

Laronzo's POV

Six weeks later…

Since that horrible night; X'avian has been staying here with me and my wife Liza and our 10-year-old daughter.

Mariah Kendranette. When Liza realized I named her after X'avian mom; she almost divorced me the same fucking day when she saw Kenda Moore's name flash in the news broadcast, the day that she was murdered.

I explained to her it was from a promise I made with Kenda long before I met her in college and got married.

We decided to tell Dranette; my daughter's nickname I gave her; the history behind her name and told her it would be her choice if she wanted to change it or not.

So, it shocked us when she said:

"I talked with X'avian and told him I felt honored to have something that was a part of his mom because it makes me feel more connected to him as a big brother, and if it would make him upset or uneasy if I kept her name; he said he was happy that I wanted to keep it and he felt she would love to share it with me."

So, she said; I'm keeping it, but she wanted to take off the Dranette and replace it with Lynn; so, now it's Mariah KendaLynn McTyson, because she felt Kendranette sounded like an old lady name; she is too smart for her age. But I love the new change.

But liza just took him in her arms and became the mother-figure he needed; but that night after she went to check on the kids, when she came back in the room; she calmly got in the bed, straddled me, leaned down in my ear, as it felt like she was reaching for my dick, as she reached in my boxers and squeezed-my-balls-like she was about to rip the mutha-fucker off as she threatened me by saying:

"If any more of your mutha-fucking skeletons come waltzing out yo Muthafucking closet; I am divorcing on the MUTHAFUCKING SPOT."

She squeezes tighter on my balls as she dig her nails deeper as she continues to say:

"And I will leave the kids with you to take while you pay me a hefty spouse support check and pay my mortgage, bills, and car notes until Mari is 21-years-old, and ya better not fuck another bitch beside me until I decide I'm ready to forgive ya stupid ass, because I know you only married me because I remind you of her."

She says this as I wonder how she found out, but answers my question when she said:

"I saw her picture that X'avian has of her in his room." She tells me and I as damn near fainted, as she squeezes even tighter on my balls, to the point it brings me to tears as she continues.

"Which-is-why, I'm doing a DNA with your son to make sure we ain't related, because I seriously look like her fucking twin and that'll make me double related to him as his maternal-aunt and step-mother thanks to your love obsession with his mother, and that also would be a whole new Pandora's box that my only parents would fucking have answers to, and put a new target on your ass from them."

She finishes as she release her fucking vice grip on my balls; which feel numb as fuck right now as she climbs off of me and went to sleep with a peaceful smile on her face.

That has me praying that they coincidentally just look alike and not actually fucking related, because she's definitely right that her parents would have questions only they have answer to.

FUCK ME BRUH!!! I knew she wasn't playing when she showed me separation and divorce papers she had our lawyer write as a warning that she wasn't playing, a week later that she kept locked away in a safe, only she knows where in our bank safe. She is definitely my ROD chick and I'm proud to call her my wife.

Vicious' POV

"Pops you ready?" I yell out to my dad as I rush down the stairs heading to the kitchen; where I find him lost in his thoughts.

"Hey mom!" I say to my stepmom Liza, as I kiss her cheek.

"Morning baby!" She responds like I'm a child, but I don't mind cause I'm use to her saying it after countless times of telling her not to call me baby.

"What's up K-Lynn!" I say to my lil sis because calling her by what the "K" stands for or her first name, still pulls on my heart strings for my mind.

"Hey Bro-Bro!" She says calling me by my pet name she gave me.

After leaving my uncle's house, as soon as we walked in the door; literally welcomed me with open arms. It took me a while to open and trust her to the point where I can call her mom. Now I wouldn't have it any other way.

Today my grandma got out of jail; my dad had the best lawyer on her case and since they had everything on tape with her confession of her involvement in the shooting. They charged her with self-defense; but had to give her some time for shooting him more than once out of anger. We cremated my uncle's body; because he left in his will that he didn't want to be buried.

His lawyer contacted my dad through his lawyers and told him that in my Unc's will he left all his gyms and money to me; that was a lot of money over 750M+ for the scholarship funds, 97M+ invested in the Celtic's team who runs the basketball camps, Patriots who run football camps and Red Sox who runs baseball camp they now dedicated all in my unc memories and the money endorsed by each team goes to the kids of his gyms. His cars and houses were given to single needy families from the local woman and children shelter to help them get back what they lost; one woman had five young kids. I gave her and her kids the house that my unc had built from the ground up for me but I know he understands why I gave it to her.

Prat agreed to continue managing the gyms with the help of my dad till I am ready to take them over, as he continue to have copartners with me when I turn 21. What my Unc didn't know; was that Prat was his-actual-half-blood brother.

Before his dad Deondrick went to prison for Cassius; no, I don't address him by his government name now because he lost that title when he confessed to having my mom murdered.

Any-who; so, Deondrick met Prat while in prison and told him he was his father when he realized Prat's last name was Azono; after a girl he had a one-night stand with in middle school before he was married to Unc's mother.

Before Prat got released; he told him about Lavon Tate and made him promise to look after him as his last dying wish. Prat got out and found out more about after reaching around the internet; basically he stalked his ass, became friends and did a sibling DNA test without my Unc knowing and turned it turned out that they were actually brothers, and he kept his father's promise, but wasn't able to tell him and show him the results because Unc went MIA before he could say anything and he didn't know; he was back in town until he heard of his death on the news.

My uncle thought he was taking him under his wing from jump, treated him like a brother-from-another-mother; if he only knew how true that statement was.

Really! It was Prat who was taking him under his wing because he was older and wanted to get to know him before he told him the truth; so let my Unc Tate think it was the other way around.

Maybe, if he would have said something sooner my Unc wouldn't have felt like he didn't have nothing to live for. I was thinking how salty I felt when he told me he was not only my Unc's BB4L aka 'Best-Bro-4-Life' but his actual brother; I was pissed at first but after I got to know him, I was finally happy to have him in my new family.

Oh, and my proudest moment is when I finally won over Ayranea, and she became my ROD chick with a little help from all the drama I was going through; she stayed by my side to keep a nigga grounded and definitely strong.

"Hey, you going to stare off in space or are you getting out the car to go pick up your grandma?"

My dad yelled at me, while snapping his finger in my face as we sit outside the police station.

Hen's POV

Since, the night me and my lil nigga had our lil-pawl-wow in front of his mom's grave he became my "Ace Boon Coon;" basically, my Day1-Nigga or for short D1N in the street's terms.

We were actually closer when he was young but after his uncle stopped coming around; I didn't want to go back to that park since I realized he wouldn't be there.

I didn't recognize him at first until my Unc clarified that he was his son and my dad mentioned him being the kid at the park. I could have flown to the moon and back; I had to make sure because I thought I was going to never see him again after he left the park.

We have been hanging out as 'Ratchet-High-Power-Couple' clique; since and Meekia, and now him and Nea are now dating; with my blessing because Nea has always been like a sis to me but now, she officially fam. Demeekia and I have been talking about getting married after high school before we leave for college. I talked about it with my dad and even though he feels we should wait, I think he caught on to the reason why.

But for now, it's just a thought in the wind.

Demeekia's POV

So, turns out prep…I mean Vicious, turned out to be my new cousin-in-law and he's not as cocky as I thought; he's actually a good peoplez with a humble spirit and fun to be around.

I can't believe that he won over Nea's stuck-up ass; he still ain't got the nookie but he doesn't seem to mind. I know why she ain't giving up but I'll be breaking our girl code if I said why she ain't giving it up till after high school, but that didn't stop her from getting down with Mrs. Carter and I. It was a one-time-deal before me and HEN hooked up; which he doesn't know but she almost let it slip out while Vicious read her ass like a book and I slipped and coughed 'Mrs. Carter.'

Darian and I relationship have gone past just a high school crush and we've been talking about getting married; even though our parents think we should wait, but it's came to a point in our life; that time has-sort-of ran-out for us....~wink-wink~

But-t-t-t; I can't say for sure.

Ayranea's POV

I love me some him; I didn't expect that the turn of events would make him my D1N. Once his family's secret fell out the closest all in one day.

I bet he didn't expect to bump into his ROD chick, walk into first class to meet his cousin; on the first day of school and reunited him with his pops; who burst open Pandora's box and have a whole unveiling of the Moore's family secrets that his grandfather tried to keep locked away from him, until his cousin found the key to open it and all his skeletons came Crip-walking out his fucking closet.

His grandfather was the cause of him to not only lose his mother but basically the rest of his family that loved and raised him: which was his grandmother; who three months later after she was released and living cozy with her new lil boo or should I say prior sidepiece of 10yrs, while still married; died with a happy soul and no, there was no foul play with her death and his Unc; who committed suicide because all of the burdens he had carried his whole life; left him to believe; he have nothing to live for, because he did his part by unveiling the truth and reconnecting X'avian with his dad.

But at the 'Repast party' where people celebrate the life you felt behind instead of mourning your death; he found out that Prat was his biological brother and his new cousin. Vicious was mad of course because he felt if his Unc would have known, he may not have felt he had nothing to live for; which could or couldn't have even been true, but Prat waited too long to say something. But after he realized that Prat's reasoning of why he waited; yo Vicious was happy he had a part of his Unc slash cousin back.

Now, it's six weeks later and we made it official; yes, I'm talking about X'avian black ass. He needed me, I helped hold him down through everything, held his hand in court during his grandma sentence, I went with him when he went to visit her and help put together her welcome home when she got of jail and she told him the truth about her double life she had in the last 10 yrs. of her marriage, with another officer in a different police precinct; half her age; a younger man who gave her the happiness and 'D' she wasn't getting from her husband that she lived with, till she died of a heart attack, and cried with him when he had to bury her.

Graduation is coming up, but I'm still going to wait until after our first year of college to give up the nookie; but, I don't mind when he gives me-my-kisses-down-low baby! Just thinking about it make me burst out singing Kelly Rowland's song: "I like my kisses down low, he makes me arch my back when he kisses it real slow"......Fuck! He has me crossing my legs on that note by just thinking how he roughly spreads my legs, inch his way down my thighs while giving me butterfly kisses, till he reaches my spot and devour my pussy like it's his last meal......

Ooh wee! The things-he-does-with his tongue got me all-hot-and-bothered. So, now I need a cold shower that note.

Damn! I hate being a virgin and shit, I may or may not give him a good Prom night.

But I guess we'll have to see, won't we?

Stay tuned for Moore

Lies Unveiled II

Coming soon!

About The Author

Shonneaita Grays (writing as Florencia Flo) and her son Va'Lad are Louisiana natives who lives up to the saying; "Home is where the heart is". Her son was the motivation she needed to move and venture out of the south to find the city in a country girl's heart and for his well-being. It was in Massachusetts where they found their home. She took to heart the theme song of Cheers: "I wanna be where everyone knows my name" and made it her own by saying: "I wanna live where nobody knows my name" because she felt Louisiana was never her forever home. A few years later she felt something was still missing from her life, but she couldn't put her finger on it until she finished reading a story from Wattpad.com; it was writing.

Writing has always been her passion and gift; she would write down her thoughts when she was angry, kept inspirational quotes and poems to comfort her. It allowed her to express herself and pour out her heart to get things off her chest so she could have a peace of mind. Just like the great authors who wrote her favorite books such as: A Day Late and a Dollar Short, Blood and Chocolate, and the many other stories from Wattpad.com. Which is where she created LouciousDiva81 and gave birth to her first book she named "Love For Money" to share with her Wattpad readers. She thought if these great writers can do it, then why can't I? She expressed her writing technique as an out-of-body experience when writing from a character POV. Her purpose is to give them life, personality, and individuality to make the readers embody the characters and be able to feel their emotions as the words paint a visual picture in their minds and she feels; that's what make her a unique writer.

To learn more about Florencia Flo and her upcoming books, visit the publishing website: www.Ajbpublishing.com